SO-AHH-524

HE STOOD TREMBLING
ON THE OCEAN'S FLOOR
AT THE EDGE OF THE WORLD

Behind him the bright shafts of sunlight played upon vividly colored fish and living reefs. Ahead lay the great chasm where the planet dropped away into eternity, where lay an unknown world.

He quivered, trying to see into that darkness, straining to read the sea's image and hear its voice. Did that black silence speak of death, or escape from death?

And then he heard it, from out of that deep, a singing, strange and modal, of almost unbearable beauty.

I will go down to her, I and none other . . .

THE MAN WHO LIVED IN INNER SPACE
by Arnold Federbush

"Beautiful . . . Closing the book, one feels as if he has just climbed out of the waves."

—Washington Post

"His conception of nature rings every bit as true as Faulkner's 'The Bear' or Hemingway's The Old Man and the Sea."

—Chicago Daily News

The Man
Who Lived
in Inner Space

Arnold Federbush

BANTAM BOOKS · TORONTO · NEW YORK · LONDON

*This low-priced Bantam Book
has been completely reset in a type face
designed for easy reading, and was printed
from new plates. It contains the complete
text of the original hard-cover edition.*
NOT ONE WORD HAS BEEN OMITTED.

RLI: $\dfrac{\text{VLM 8 (VLR 8–9)}}{\text{IL 9–adult}}$

THE MAN WHO LIVED IN INNER SPACE
*A Bantam Book / published by arrangement with
the author*

PRINTING HISTORY
Houghton Mifflin edition published February 1973
Bantam edition / May 1975

All rights reserved.
Copyright © 1973 by Bantam Books, Inc.
*This book may not be reproduced in whole or in part, by
mimeograph or any other means, without permission.
For information address: Bantam Books, Inc.*

Published simultaneously in the United States and Canada

*Bantam Books are published by Bantam Books, Inc. Its trade-
mark, consisting of the words "Bantam Books" and the por-
trayal of a bantam, is registered in the United States Patent
Office and in other countries. Marca Registrada. Bantam
Books, Inc., 666 Fifth Avenue, New York, New York 10019.*

PRINTED IN THE UNITED STATES OF AMERICA

1 The old elevated highway was built to carry traffic over the river and swamps that bordered the city. Since then the swamps have been filled in, but there is a new benefit. Certain offensive industries were drawn to the river even as they were prohibited within the city. The visitor can drive right over this grim area, euphemistically called an industrial park, and need never know it exists. He will be more likely to look out across the picturesque city itself, set on the slopes of several rolling hills as if on a medieval tapestry. It is a particularly striking sight when the fog comes rolling in from the Pacific and the city seems to rise above the clouds.

At odd moments in his driving the visitor will catch glimpses of the ocean, perhaps with the sunlight streaking across it as if off some great silver sword, silhouetting the numerous ships that utilize the natural harbor. The elevation will cut off any view of the beaches to the south but the driver will be reminded they are there because of countless photographs and paintings of that especially beautiful area, usually of strange rocks set amidst foaming surf, or of waves thrown high against sheer cliff walls. If the visitor has time he may get to see those seascapes for himself and he will not be disappointed.

All in all, he will be greatly impressed with this first viewing, and it will confirm what he has always been led to believe about the loveliness of the city.

Occasionally, however, he may get stopped by a clanging sound and flashing lights as he approaches the river crossing. A rusted gate will creak noisily down, blocking his way, and huge iron wheels on the steel towers will clank and squeal as they lift the roadway span to allow some barge through. Inevitably the visitor will be upset at the slowness with which it all happens—certainly it takes longer than a freight train at a railroad crossing. If it is summer and his car carries no air-conditioning, he will curse the heat.

He will look anxiously at his watch, then at the gauges on his car, particularly at the temperature which will be approaching a discomforting level. He may then look below to the river yearning for a cooling swim, and have a brief reminiscence of younger days and cleaner waters, but one closer look at this river will cut short that reverie.

He will turn back to the chugging barge to find it has made astonishingly little progress, barely halfway past the bridge. Since he can see it more clearly now, he will note it carries tanks of obviously dangerous gases or fuels, or piles of solid wastes to dump out at sea.

There will still be plenty of time before that barge passes and now he will honk his horn out of sheer frustration; perhaps in the wild fancy the honking will awaken the captain out of his stupor, he will rev up the diesel engines into high gear, and the barge will speed off with spume flying.

It will not happen of course, and now the visitor's gaze drifts ahead of the barge, following the river's course upstream until he sees what the Chamber of Commerce was hoping he would not see. First will come the strange colors, the foams and sludges emptying right into the water from numerous pipes, and from there his scornful gaze will rise to nightmarish forms vaguely suggestive of the Orient, the catalytic towers like Arab minarets, the electrical insulators like Chinese pagodas. Then, following the power lines strung between steel towers like sagging clotheslines, he will come to blackened chimneys pouring out hot gases that set the air above shimmering, then to industrial graveyards with the remains of autos and unrecognizable rubble.

Some yards stack piles of steel cylinders, and for a moment the visitor will find relief from the gray landscape in the cheery bright colors, but then he will remember they are codes for the dark contents—acetylene, naptha, methane, propane. Weaving between and among them are steel rails with freight cars shuttling their deadly cargo from spurs to a locomotive on a main line, or to barges on the river.

His eye will finally fall on the source of it all, the factories themselves, low brick slabs commingling with stubby steel spheres, all together producing the pollutions that glut the land, air, and water about them.

Who could possibly inhabit and run such a plant? Perhaps a worker as deformed and ugly as the surroundings, some gnome cackling fiendishly as he opens the sluice gate to pour more evil liquids into the river.

To the driver ecology is the issue of his time, and he pictures himself a hero dynamiting the factories in a midnight commando raid and saving the world from pollution. But then the fantasy fades to a more practicable form—starting a petition to close down these festering eyesores for good, or, more likely, signing one if it happens to come his way.

By now the barge will have passed, the drawbridge settled, and he will step hard on the gas pedal to make up for lost time and get away faster from this ugliness.

"Lovely."

Colin looked out the grimy window at the barge chugging slowly past, while above him the traffic sped across the drawbridge. He wiped away some more grime with his sleeve and looked out across the river at the other chemical plants, their dirtied walls crowding out a good deal of the sky and sunlight, and certainly any view of the city beyond.

The other engineers and technicians looked up astonished, but Colin was too busy at the window to notice. He followed the power lines down to the storage tanks and rubble-filled yards, and then to the spewing vents and pipelines. "Absolutely incredible."

Then he became aware of the eyes in the room staring at him and turned around to meet them. "Haven't you ever looked?"

They were gathered at the windowless end of the room, near the vending machines, and it was evident that in years of coffee breaks no one had looked at all.

"I liked the view better when I couldn't see it," said the supervisor.

"Or smell it," added a second.

"Don't remind me," said the supervisor. "My wife reminds me, my kids remind me, the papers remind me. But right now I'd like to have my coffee in peace."

Stung, Colin started to speak, but the engineer held up his hand in a gesture indicating he didn't want to hear another word, and the second engineer emphasized it: "The chief is lousy to work for if he hasn't had his coffee in peace."

Colin glanced at the clock. Only ten-thirty. His first day was going to be a long one.

But what had he said wrong? He respected the silence as long as he could, but he soon realized it wouldn't get him any closer to the people with whom he would be working. He took another risk.

"Uh . . . supposing I say cheering things, and make tomorrow's round of drinks on me?"

The chief shrugged.

"Years ago they were burning iron pyrites to get rid of the sulfur, and the sulfur dioxide fumes seared the green right off the Tennessee mountains, burned out the whole countryside a lot worse than anything outside that window. But then we found what sulfur dioxide was worth—explosives first, then fertilizer, then ..."

"So?"

"So when the waste became more valuable than the product, that solved it. Now what we're pouring out there ..."

"You got a use for it?"

"Well no, but with some more basic research we can come up with a few things, and ..."

"And then all that garbage out there, poof, gone! Right kid?"

"Well, not in a poof, maybe, but ..."

"Yah, all right. So you come up with a brainstorm that founds ten new industries, but then what about the wastes of those ten, and then ten times the ten?"

"Well, part of the challenge's tying them back in so the waste of the last one is the raw material for the first."

The supervisor snorted. "The kid's got it all figured out,

a closed system, each plant fuels another." Then he smiled. "Well, it doesn't fuel me."

That started something and one technician in back of the room called out, "There's no fuel like an old fuel." The engineers groaned.

Said another, "Hows' about, 'One plant's heat is another plant's poison.' " The groans grew louder.

"Well," said Colin, "your jokes are lousy, but they're still right. A closed system's still feasible."

"No," began another, "because you can fuel some of the feas'ble some of the time, but you can't fuel all ..." and the supervisor cut him off.

"Sure, it's feasible. In a million years, maybe. The trouble is you've gotta tie in everything. *Everything,* because anything left over'll pile up like it's piled outside that window. That means I can't smoke a cigar without you figuring in the smoke."

Colin was perplexed. He had expected he needed only make his suggestion and set the whole room buzzing with excitement and ideas. He certainly had no defense ready, never having expected a war. Finally he answered with a wan smile, "Well, cigars aren't healthy for you anyway."

He heard a few derisive snickers, and one technician cat-called, "Louder and funnier!"

All eyes were on the supervisor, who seemed to enjoy the moment. He puffed on his cigar and finally said, "Smart-ass grads who're gonna change the world by Tuesday don't help my blood pressure either."

The others enjoyed the remark as much as he did. Colin reddened, but held his temper, hoping to gain rapport despite the signs. "But it's got to start somewhere."

"Why start what you know you won't finish in a million years? Especially when you've got a career to push."

"A lotta garbage'll pile up in a million years."

"In a million years I'll worry."

Colin looked again at the others in the room, seeking one friend among them. "The rest of you see it that way?"

They shrugged, and one of them added aloud, "Only the chief'll live a million years to see it anyway."

There was a round of chuckles and smiles and then, bored with it all, they went back to their own private conversations and thoughts. Colin finally turned his attention back out the window, more glum than before. He realized he would never see the same view they did. He knew they were tired, hemmed in by time payments and mortgages to jobs with shrinking markets and faster-shrinking respect.

And out the window lay the reminder of it all.

But Colin saw a different view, as exciting to him as it was depressing to them. Already he started analyzing the component chemicals of that rubble, mulling over possible new uses. Then suddenly he felt he was wasting his time staring out the window and dreaming when the resources and tools lay just upstairs, with only one lifetime in which to learn how to use them.

"Well ..." he said aloud, "a million years. I'd better get hustling on it." He swallowed his last gulp of coffee, crushed the cup in the wastebasket, and was out the door in almost a single smooth motion, with the words over his shoulder of "Call me for lunch."

A moment later the engineers heard his clatter on the stairs.

"Good God, listen to that. He actually can't wait."

"He's a kid, a goddam naive kid."

They thought back on their own fresh-out-of-school days when they had their own dreams, and their lives seemed wide-open roads with any number of enticing turns. Then they remembered how the roads narrowed, their options seemed to close off and the dreams faded.

"Wait'll he's had a few years' seasoning. He'll learn."

They were silent again, and the supervisor took another swallow of the coffee that suddenly seemed cold and stale.

Colin was anxious to know every inch of the plant thoroughly, so he wandered along the catwalk matching compressors, pumps, and pipelines against the flow sheet on his clipboard. He stopped by the storage tanks: acetylene, naphtha, methane, propane . . .

These were the deadly chemicals that tainted the air, scorched the earth, curdled the water, and could explode any time in a devastating catastrophe. Yet they were the basics of medicines and metals, printing inks and plastics, and an almost endless list of bounties to strike dumb the ancient alchemists.

Lead into gold? Take the sulfur from the iron pyrites to make sulfuric acid. Add chlorine from seawater and acetylene from coal. Mix corrosives with explosives, danger with peril, and what do you get? Acetylsalicylic acid. Aspirin.

He would be dealing with the same elements the ancients dealt with, earth, air, water, and fire, and his transformations would shame them. The wastes outside would be broken back into these chemicals and he would build new molecules, new miracles. All things were possible, beginning with the contents of those tanks.

Then Colin traced the path of the river-intake line and checked the gauges to see that it flowed properly. "Keep them cool," he said, pleasantly patting the large pipeline. The sleeping beasts in the tanks had to be kept sleeping, some of them at temperatures below zero.

For years before Colin had come the river had served that function, carrying away the heat generated in the chemical reactions, but in those years other plants had been drawn to the river. It was a raw material for a number of their processes, provided some power and transportation, but its use as a coolant was certainly the most important, and each plant diverted a heavy amount of river water for just that purpose.

Of course that meant the river was getting warmer. That could hardly have been anticipated years ago when this particular plant had the river practically to itself, so no account was taken of it, no special gauges or safety devices installed, and now inside a steel tank temperatures rose and a beast that had slept for years was slowly waking.

Colin picked up the nearby telephone and asked for an outside line. He dialed and waited several rings.

"Hello," said a sleepy girl's voice.

"Hello," said Colin.

He heard her sudden breath. "Hello," she said again, but in a very, very different tone. They didn't say anything more for a good long while but just listened to each other's breathing and imagined they were touching as they had been just a few hours before.

"What're you doing?" he asked finally.

"Missing you. What're you doing?"

"Oh, miracles—"

"Yeh, name two."

"Give me time. I'm just coming off my coffee break. But soon, soon." He looked at the steel tanks and thought of the wonders the contents could be molded into.

He did not see through the steel to the warming liquid inside, sloughing off molecules into the air to form a vapor, growing heavy and rich with surrounding oxygen until a mysterious point was being reached where heat, fuel, and air would devastatingly fuse.

If he had seen, he would have forgotten dreams and musings, dropped the phone and run until his heart pounded and his legs buckled, and then he would have crawled desperately until the skin on his fingers tore. He would not have bothered to shut switches and valves, and in his panic he would even have forgotten to warn his colleagues. In that quickest and deepest instinct his only thought would have been for his own life.

"I've got a few notions," he said to his girl. "A molded plastic house, harder than steel, lighter than wood, mildewproof, insectproof, insulated, fine at the poles or the equator. Mass-produced for, say fifty dollars."

"Ha. When and where?"

"I don't know when, but where—it'll start right here," and he knocked on the tanks so she could hear.

Inside the tank was something she did not hear, but would. It remained small at first, placidly sucking in molecules of air and fuel, but growth made it ravenous. As the air molecules were pulled close, it leaped across them like steppingstones, consuming them as it went and growing larger.

"I'll give you more than two miracles. Nonpolluting fertilizers that'll multiply yield a dozen times, or a dozen hundred times. We've got three-dollar radios, why not three-dollar TVs? Or mini hi-fis? Everybody in the world can finally hear Mozart."

"Everybody in the world won't like Mozart."

"Then I'm not going to give them their three-dollar TVs."

Within the tank a disturbance grew to a turbulence, a ripple into a wave, groping in an ever-widening circle, carrying raging heat and energy as it raced out beyond its breeding place. It pushed molecules of air before it, grabbing the near ones, lifting them on its crest, searing them with its intense heat until they shuddered and broke apart, adding the heat and energy they gave off to its own, growing stronger and hotter, more virulent as the moments passed.

No gauges reacted, no alarms. Downstairs some engineers dawdled over their coffee longer than usual.

"Of course," said Colin, "I'd have to find electronics people with the same ambitions. Then, let's see. You know what problems they had mass-producing penicillin? There are some thousand-dollar medicines crying for mass production ideas. There's too much to do. Why should I spend my time talking to you?"

"Well, why are you?"

"You called my bluff." Already, however, he was beginning to feel anxious over the time he was losing. His mind wandered to the problems of mass-produced medicines and he wondered if there were biochemists he could talk to. He regretted not having taken more biology courses. He was silent a good while, and she wondered where he had gone.

Free particles of air at the periphery of the tank were crowded together as the wave came closer, pushing them against the wall. The steel shuddered, but its strongly bonded molecules recovered and held. Then the full force of the wave struck, doubling the pressure, then doubling it again. The heat was so intense the bondings sagged and grew weaker. Already Colin heard the first screams of the steel as it tore apart, and knew it was too late.

"Colin! ..." and her voice was drowned in an explosion bursting its prison, heaving its fragments wide. The wave swept Colin into itself, lifted him as easily as it had lifted mere molecules, spun him on its crest, and sent him crashing down on twisted steel beams.

He gripped the phone tightly, imagining it for a moment to be her hand, and so his thoughts were outside himself at that moment and he watched his body die (or was his brain deceiving him as it absorbed the narcotic gases?).

The wave shriveled the small hairs on his skin and then

seared the numerous cells beneath, layer after layer, millions of them in a square inch.

As heat attacked the skin, the shock wave attacked the bones, rending center shafts in jagged splinters that flew through surrounding muscle, ripping apart canals of blood vessels like some cataclysmic quake upon a great city.

The wave pushed on to the shiny ligaments that bridged bone to bone and snapped them one at a time until the whole bridge collapsed, bringing down soft red muscles, white tendons, bundles of striped fibers, thin elastic membranes, and among them more billions of living vessels.

The impulse to scream ran through nerves to the proper muscles, and when he opened his mouth, heated gases rushed in through throat and voice box, snaking around the labyrinths of air passages, dividing as the windpipe itself divided, branching out to reach all parts of the unprotected lungs.

Then came the aftermath. Like rains running unchecked through a burned-out forest, waters began flooding his burned body. Half his weight was water, and the fluids had been kept in balance and distributed by delicate mechanisms. Now those mechanisms had gone awry and unexpelled liquids broke through. In the skin, straw-colored lymph raced beneath the burned areas, puffing layers of skin up in great blisters.

Around the bones the fluids had kept tissues watered, joints lubricated. Now rushing waters filled newly formed craters to a bursting point.

The lungs should have thrown off the fluids collecting there, but instead they were drowning helplessly in the accumulations, and Colin was drowning with them. Though in the midst of impossibly dry hot gases, he was dying from flood, from water.

Breaths now came in pained gushes, coughs to force back the gases, wheezes to bring in bits of precious oxygen through membranes inflamed and clogged with fluids.

He was drowning in his own sea.

Even in what he sensed was a mind wandering as it neared death, Colin heard each cell, gland, vessel scream as it died, billions upon countless billions, each a living thing, each sacred, each living out its life to serve him. He, himself, dying while he gasped, wheezed, choked, and drowned, all in a pain that seemed to wrench his very soul out of its socket.

He heard his heart race feverishly, fighting approaching death until it too weakened, slowed, became irregular and confused, wandered away.

Puzzles left unsolved, wonders he would never know, creations uncreated, dreams undreamt, a girl he loved who loved him, and finally the universe within him flooded in a sea, each inhabitant screaming as it died.

... drowning ...

Now that dark sea reached his mind and he saw the blackness close in on the edges. Dimly he saw shapes, strange shadows approaching, distant voices echoing. Then the sea closed in and swamped him.

And then, nothing.

2 "All right, all right, hold on!"

The unhearing telephone rang on insistently.

Colin reached for his crutches, and blistered skin pulled against his every motion with a ferocious itching. He gasped as he drew himself up and the deep breaths set ulcered lungs against inflamed membranes. He finally worked the crutches under his arms and strained atrophied muscle.

The telephone rang on.

"I'm coming, damn it!" He tottered to his feet and stood trembling on ruptured cartilage. Pitted, twisted joints cramped every forward move. He had never gotten used to it. Twenty years after the accident, long after ravaged bone and tissue had been scarred over, his body was still a torture.

Gasping and cursing, he reached for the phone.

"Hello. Plant."

"This is the office. We've a batch of orders here, so if you'll switch to data transmission we'll send 'em through."

Colin switched the phone to data transmission and in moments the machine was printing out long rows of numbers. Colin sniffed as he watched, recognizing the numbers as more aspirins for more headaches, more photo film for more vacationers, more detergents for more dirty people.

He sighed as he tore off the paper, hobbled to the various controls, and set them in accordance with the new specifications. Almost immediately the computer made the adjustments to the factory below. Pumps, agitators, furnaces, cooling towers all responded like massive organ pipes to a toccata on the keyboard, a music of an increasing clatter at a higher pitch.

From his booth he could see the entire factory, though he rarely cared to. He didn't see outside but knew the outlet pipes would be emptying more effluents into the river.

The computer not only directed the machines but monitored them minutely. The slightest difference in temperature or rate of flow or pressure was quickly detected and automatically adjusted faster than Colin could have. That of course was why it had been installed after the accident. The operation that once required a good number of people could now be maintained by one, and even he did little more than generally supervise the largely self-sufficient plant.

Still, pushing buttons was a better fate than being hidden away to vegetate in some dark corner of a sanatorium.

The telephone rang again.

"Hello. Plant."

It was another complaint. You people are pouring an awful lot of dirty liquid into the river. Can't you do something?

The voice was strangely familiar and so were the words. It was a few moments before Colin realized it was almost his own words and voice twenty years before, and when he answered he felt he was almost talking to his own younger self. He handled his caller with tact, explaining the difficulties of a "closed system." He was reminded once more of what he must have sounded like twenty years ago, a young fool.

Yet why this aching, this sense of things lost? Why this wish to be a fool, a child to whom all roads seemed open, all miracles possible?

But of course they weren't. Aging and maturity taught there were no magical solutions to painful problems.

Children are fools, and fools are children, and that is all there is to it.

He felt suddenly weary and decided he could use a coffee break so he let himself down the stairs, one painful step at a time, to the room below. Twenty years ago it had served as the lounge for the engineers and technicians, but it had since been converted to living quarters for him. He had spent all these years shuttling between lounge and factory and it had worked out well enough.

A small kitchen replaced the vending machine, and the usual spare furnishings took up the rest of the space, except for an abundance of books and tapes soon to be supplemented with a film projector. And one living thing, a well-tended potted fern.

The window through which Colin had looked twenty years before was grimier than ever, now nearly opaque.

Not that Colin minded. He had no more desire to look than his old colleagues. In fact the view would have been worse than ever. Other plants had since been built along the riverbank, and their wastes thickened the river and darkened the sky even more.

He paused at the bottom of the stairs to rest, massaged his legs and back, rubbed a specially prescribed lotion on his skin, and when the pain persisted he turned to his most soothing balm, to music.

He thumbed past tapes of the familiar pieces, the warm harmonies and restrained rhythms most thought of as Mozartean. Instead he turned to the strange and haunted Mozart of the nineteenth quartet, the "Dissonant," and sat back in his one soft chair to listen.

A cello began with a throbbing that matched his own, then one by one the instruments built a chord that seemed the essence of pain. What was the inspiration of those excruciating sounds that other composers would not touch for another century? What grimy window did Mozart clear away to see a future landscape no one else could see?

Two minutes later it was gone, the strange vision vanished, the window opaque again. The composer died too young, before he could follow that vision again, his dreams undreamt, puzzles unsolved, the creations uncreated, and Colin grieved.

The second movement, Andante Cantabile, slow and sweetly songful, a love song that reminded him of her, brought back to him the face he once caressed and the body he held, and yearned now to touch again. He could not forget, though certainly she had forgotten him.

Tears. She had come to him when he lay dying and had cried for him. But then he didn't die. The medical miracles that had saved him from drowning in his own fluids could not help the ravages of that flood, and he was left with a body ugly beyond tolerance and certainly beyond love.

So when he persisted in living, her tears gradually lessened, love became pity, and then a greater pity for herself. Finally even she, even she no longer came to see him.

Colin's gaze drifted about his room and stopped on the telephone. He remembered how it once seemingly brought her close to him, but afterward it became an excuse for her distance. Finally she did not call at all, and when he did another man answered and told him not to call again.

Even as he knew she had forgotten him, some dim hope refused to die and tormented him now.

Tears! Damned lying crocodile tears.

And still that tiny bit of hope persisted.

The telephone rang. Then a second time and a third.

He stilled the music, and shook with an added trembling as he pulled himself to his feet, desperately afraid the caller would hang up before he reached the phone, but it rang on in the silence. "Please ... please ..."

He lunged for it at too great a distance and fell. He straightened himself against the wall and took a breath before daring to speak. "H ... hello?"

It was another complaint.

This time he slammed the receiver down in a rage, and turned up the music again as the quartet reached the final movement. Andante gave way to Allegro, the song to a dance, and Colin was eased.

Pain was soon left behind. He was not alone in the world. He had Mozart and he had guests who would soon be coming, good friends who were neither deceitful nor fools.

Humming along with the music, even pausing to conduct a few bars, he made his way to the refrigerator for the bin of food he had been saving. He divided the portions onto several plates and carried them all out the door to the yard outside where he called out, clanging a knife against a dish.

There was a silence at first and Colin looked about him, at first puzzled and then disturbed. His Mozart faded. Then he spotted something and brightened again.

"Come on," he called out to his first shy guest. "Come on."

From a hole underneath a cylinder, a cat crept out slowly and looked suspiciously across at Colin.

"That's it ... I won't hurt you ... C'mon."

The cat was thin and scraggly, evidently starving. Still it was in no rush to approach, its hunger matched by its wariness. It crept toward Colin with utmost caution.

Then a dog showed itself, emerging from the darkness of an alleyway, quite as thin and badly scratched.

"You too. Come on."

Several more cats and dogs came out of their lairs, all old beyond their years.

They approached their plates and ate slowly and quietly, each from its own plate.

Colin leaned down to pat them, but they felt only a thief's hand and recoiled. He backed off and watched them from several feet away as they finished and returned to their separate lairs.

Colin stood alone in the yard. The air was heavy with the rancid smell of the river.

So now he was alone again, to spend the rest of his life as he had spent most of his years so far, while the world spun on without him, making its way with its triumphs and disasters, and his existence contributing and detracting no more than some insect or pebble.

Why bother then with this pain of living at all? It would be easy enough to end it. Methane, propane, acetylene ... those sleeping beasts could be awakened easily enough with a few turns of a control.

He stopped the thought before it crystallized. He had already come close to death and learned it was far worse than any agony of living.

If only he weren't so alone ...

But who? And where?

He looked up at his one room and the plant that had been his home, and across to the others that had marked his boundaries. Above him the traffic clattered across the old drawbridge and sped on into the city.

The city. He remembered a place where there were others, and a possible companion among them.

He hesitated. It had been a good many years ...

He took a breath and put his crutches forward, stiffening

as the blisters stung his skin, drew himself up with a shudder as his weakened bones caught his weight.

He had taken the first step. A hundred more and he reached the highway. He turned west underneath, following in its shadow to the city.

He could almost believe they were waiting there to welcome him.

3 The elevated highway ran through the business and industrial sections, and the people fleeing to the suburbs at the workday's end did not notice the gnomish figure hobbling in the darkness below, nor did Colin wish to be noticed so he kept to the shadows.

The sun was low near the city's hills by the time Colin reached the park. It was in a now-decrepit neighborhood, and the lengthening shadows emphasized the gloom. The once carefully tended greenery was overrun with weeds in some places, and dying in muddy brown patches in others. Benches and other fixtures that were long ago vandalized or weathered were simply left to rot. The city had burst its seams in other directions, and its money went elsewhere.

No one now came to this unpleasant place, but Colin's uneasiness was eclipsed by his increasing excitement as he approached his goal.

Then he saw it up ahead, just as he remembered it, or almost so. The great iron gate was battered and badly rusted but he could still discern the artwork and knew it still held its promise. There were representations of primates, birds, big cats, reptiles, and so on, indicating the abundance of animals that awaited inside.

As he pushed through the gate he thought it strange that the zoo didn't seem to be much of an attraction, but whatever the reason it was to Colin's advantage. He could roam freely and unself-consciously with no concern for the stares of others.

The smaller walks branched out in numerous directions to many promising buildings and courts, and for a moment Colin was dizzy wondering where to begin.

Well, he could start at the top of the hill with the primates. They were the most intelligent, the most humanlike of the creatures, a fact of nature which the sign outside the ape house confirmed.

"Man has always felt an affinity for these intelligent creatures . . ." The rest was too rusted to read but it was a good beginning. His own family was certainly the best.

He pushed open the door and announced his presence in a loud clear voice, but there was no chatter nor were there growls or whatever answers of welcome Colin expected. There was no sound at all.

Puzzled and annoyed, Colin dragged himself past the cages and looked in briefly at each one. They were empty and only rusty signs remained to tell who once lived there . . . SPIDER MONKEY . . . WOOLLY MONKEY . . . BARBARY APE . . . LOWLAND GORILLA . . . PYGMY CHIMPANZEE . . .

Well, it didn't matter all that much. It was still a big zoo with plenty of places left to visit. On his way out he noticed the weathered sign pointing to the birdhouse.

Birds. Certainly more his type than primates if one thought about it, once one got past the superficial dissimilarity, that is, and looked to the inner spirit. Maybe his body was grounded but his mind could soar. A bird was really much more of a soul mate.

The smaller birds would be in separate cages, each with its own barely readable sign:

. . . GREAT HORNED OWL . . . IVORY-BILLED WOODPECKER . . . RUBY-THROATED HUMMINGBIRD . . . GOLDEN ORIOLE . . .

He expected a wide variety of sounds. Owls alone were capable of screams, hoots, snorts, coughs, hisses. But the cages were silent.

Steel netting was strung over huge curving arches to form the giant birdcage, and the identifying signs bore drawings to help the visitor pick out his favorite from the melee within. Or what was once a melee. Now the drawings were only a reminder.

. . . WHOOPING CRANE . . . EUROPEAN FLAMINGO . . . BALD EAGLE . . . GREAT BLUE HERON . . . PEREGRINE FALCON . . .

Reptiles.

*Turtles have been on this earth for 175 million years
... But apparently not this year.*

*Lizards not only creep and slither; some can run at
blurry speed.* None crept, slithered, or ran.

Suddenly, unexpectedly, there was an inhabited cage.
Colin almost bypassed it for all he saw was a pile of dead
wood and imitation leaves. A moment later, however, one
of the twigs came alive, flicked its tongue to test the air,
and then the entire intricately twisted branch slithered
across the gravel toward Colin, unwinding in a straight line
as it came.

Colin stared, hypnotized by its simultaneous ugliness and
beauty, a creature much like himself. The snake reached
the glass barrier and stopped, as if having displayed its one
great trick it now awaited applause. Surely it was worthy at
least of respect, this most subtle, most crafty of creatures.

In ages past it crept through graveyards and so was
thought to carry the accumulated wisdom of all the dead
souls. It guarded the Tree of Knowledge and the treasure
of Apollo. It rose high on the crowns of kings and wound
itself round the doctor's staff, all to show the bearer carried
wisdom.

Now it offered Colin the serenity that comes with
knowledge of the meaning of life and death, and Colin was
tempted.

Then he stopped. Colin had two crippled legs but the
snake had none. He hobbled but the snake crawled, not to
mention its bad skin and general all-around ugliness. Wisdom wasn't worth that much. Colin could do better.

He went on to the lion house. Here were the genuine
lords of forest and jungle, regal, powerful, graceful. He
searched eagerly past the empty cages.

... AFRICAN LION ... SIBERIAN TIGER ... SNOW LEOP-
ARD ... OCELOT ... CHEETAH ... PUMA ... JAGUAR ...

"Well, hello."

The lynx stopped taking the measure of her cage and
looked at Colin to take his measure. She approached the
bars and studied him with interest.

If she was interested, he was entranced. The lynx's sleek
body with bobbed tail, her slender face with ears streamlined to points combined to make her the most exquisite of

the great cats. Even in confinement she embodied speed, power, and grace.

What was it like to have four good legs, to bound through forgotten forests in the exhilaration of the hunt?

There was a time man knew, a long-ago age when he regarded himself as simply one more animal among many, even envying their strengths. At that time man sensed his likeness to them, that they were made from the same life substance, the spirit protoplasm that differed only in the outer shell. Underneath they were brothers and if a man could change that outer shell he would be transformed. He would have the flight of the eagle, the strength of the bear, the stamina of the wolf.

He would go through a ritual to bring himself in touch with the occult forces. He would change his outer shell and wear the animal's feathers or fur. He would imitate its ways in song and dance. The spirit protoplasm would move within him and he would be transformed into a man-eagle, a man-bear, a man-wolf.

Perhaps it was still possible, even here, even now. The same protoplasm still ran in both man and beast. If Colin wished it deeply enough he might find his way back to that time. He could partake of the sacred ritual and work the ancient spells. He could be a man-lynx.

He hobbled closer, as close as the railing allowed and came closer to those crafty cat eyes that caught the glints of the sun, bounced them within and returned them magnified. The green rims dazzled, but the centers held a darkness that seemed to pull Colin into timeless depths.

It was still possible . . .

Then the lynx yawned, thoroughly bored. She stretched and scratched at the floor, and finally settled down into a nap.

Colin sighed.

He came last to the plaza of the big animals who should have been not only survivors but victors. Surely here . . .

. . . AFRICAN ELEPHANT . . . GRIZZLY BEAR . . . BACTRIAN CAMEL . . . The bars were rusted, the concrete cracked.

. . . GIRAFFE . . . HIPPOPOTAMUS . . . RHINOCEROS . . .

A soft wind blew newspapers along the edges and against the bars.

There was nothing further here for him and he turned homeward, passing the free-form stonework of the seal pool, now crumbling and empty of water. A seal pup lay there lethargically and picked its head up as Colin passed. He barely noticed.

The common seal lacked the attractiveness of its better-known circus-star cousin, the sea lion. It was the sea lion with its sleek coat and long graceful head and neck that was always given the main pool at the zoo, being the fairer attraction.

This seal was even uglier than most. Out of water, too young for its blubber to have formed, but with its infant fur beginning to molt, the pup resembled a ragged bolster, its white fur wearing away in patches revealing the dirty gray stuffing underneath.

The pup scratched the ground with comic little claws at the end of its flippers as it crawled after Colin. A remnant of a tail protruded out between its trailing hind legs. It cried out *maaa*, hungry for the food and affection denied it by a careless keeper, but pathetic as it sounded to Colin, he was in no mood to give either.

"Beat it!"

Its eyelids were without lashes, the ears mere round holes. Only the eyes could be called beautiful. They were large, round, deeply expressive, and they showed clear melancholia. Now, incredibly, tears formed at their corners and ran down the seal's cheeks in little rivulets.

Tears! Not again, not this time!

The tears enraged him beyond measure. He lifted a crutch and banged it on the bars. *"Stop pestering me!"*

Frightened, she now showed the most telling difference between her and the sea lion. The latter had four good solid flippers on the ground, could walk readily if clumsily, and even manage a gallop at times. But this seal pup's legs dragged behind, flat and useless. She had to crawl by pulling herself forward on her front flippers and dragging her body up afterward like some inchworm ... or as Colin suddenly recognized, like himself.

He looked about him. Nothing. No one.

He lifted the latch and opened the gate for her. She crawled out readily.

The zoo was probably glad to be rid of her, Colin felt. Outside, the traffic sped busily by on the highway above. No one noticed the strangely comic, strangely touching sight of two cripples leaving the zoo and hobbling home together.

4 She was thin and flaccid, nearly dead of starvation, but still she would throw away all the fish he offered her, even when he tried to push it down her throat. Instead she would bite him and bawl louder in hunger.

He soon learned that though seals ate fish, a young pup had to be fed far more elaborately—and messily. Colin had to prepare a milk fattened with liberal amounts of margarine and cod liver oil. Then he had to pump it directly into a howling, fighting seal, running a long rubber tube all the way to the bottom of her stomach. Only then did she fall quiet and still.

This way she gained several pounds a day until she was a furry plump pup, living in a wooden pen in the yard. However that furry plumpness only seemed to worsen an ill-wrought anatomy. Weak front flippers strained at pulling a puffy body with heavy and useless rear flippers. Her loose-hanging flesh and thick fur trapped her body heat and chafed her skin. Knowing no other life, though, she accepted this misfit one.

One morning Colin used the milk to lead her into the chemical plant, to the edge of a huge vat filled with a strange quivering substance.

"There. Like it?"

She sniffed at it curiously.

"For swimming, drinking, whatever else seals do."

He nudged her closer, almost to the edge. She yelped and backed away, shivering in fright.

"It's nice, clear, cool unpolluted water, filtered at great expense and trouble, because I like you. Here . . ."

He leaned down and splashed some on her. She greeted

this with a new sound, a bearlike growl, and there was no mistaking her emotion.

He sighed. She needed help, that was all, just a little push.

He pushed gently, but she growled and backed off further.

Then he leaned back on his crutches and shoved her in.

It was a substance unlike any she had ever felt. It was as if the solid earth itself had given way beneath her. It reached up, wrapped itself around and encircled her, tried to pull her down into its bowels.

She splashed at it feverishly with her tiny front flippers, setting up a pitiable wail and trying to climb up the side of the tank, only to meet Colin's crutch pushing her back in.

"Come on. Enjoy it."

Again she tried to climb up the side, and this time he pushed her firmly all the way to the center of the tank. "Come on. Splash around from there. It's fun, I tell you."

She splashed ever more frantically, trying to keep her head above the surface. As the water soaked through her fur it made her heavier until finally she could no longer fight. Little by little she sank further until only her black nose showed. Then, in a reflex action, the nostrils closed tight and she sank slowly, still as death, until she touched bottom and lay there inert.

This was not what Colin had expected.

He stood cowering at the edge and now saw what had made her afraid. He pictured himself jumping into the tank to save her. The water would give way beneath him. He would flail and fight as she had done to stay above it until he too finally tired and drowned.

Now she lay so herself at the bottom of the tank. And he had done this to her.

He began to weep.

Then something happened. Slowly that corpse began to rise as if it had sloughed off some heavy anchor. It rose until the nose broke surface. The nostrils opened and she took a couple of deep breaths; they closed again, and again she sank slowly.

This time she hovered halfway between surface and bottom, relaxing in buoyancy felt for the first time, cradled into deep rest.

At last her flippers moved, and she seemed a feather stirred by a gust of wind.

She tried again, and again she stirred. She was indeed feather-light and would not fall or drown. She moved her flippers more strongly and darted several feet. She was no longer a prisoner of her body. One by one, dormant muscles and responses were awakened, and she realized this was the medium she was born to.

With energetic strokes of her flippers she could swim the length of the tank. She dived to the bottom ... then to the surface, trying out the places of least resistance, of greatest control. Her rear flippers, useless appendages and dead weight on land, here felt light and powerful. She bent them back and forth like a mated pair of sculling oars and glided easily. She put her front flippers to her side and found they fitted neatly into their own depressions, increasing her speed.

She spread her flippers out again. They were wings to steer and bank. She could shoot to the end of the tank and turn at the last moment ... or she could plane upward and swerve down.

The body that sagged on land like a slug here molded itself to her purpose. It could grow inches to become a sleek arrow, or could bend as she wished, taking a curve by becoming the curve itself.

She flew more easily than the birds, for they had to fight the weight of air and beat their wings to simply stay aloft. But she was lighter than the fluid about her, and this gave her the full freedom of her body.

She added variations, intricate baroque decorations, banks, turns, rolls, loops in combinations, ever more intricate and complex.

She broke the surface and snorted excitedly, then clambered up the side of the tank and pulled on Colin's leg. "Oh no," he said, "you're not getting me in there. Here's my home."

He returned to the usual day's dreary work, except for occasional glances at her frolicking in the tank. Then he would wistfully imagine himself equally free, the lynx bounding across the forest.

If he wished it deeply enough ...

Already as he closed his eyes he felt his legs grow strong, his arms stretch to become forepaws, the faint scent of passing prey setting nerves quivering, muscles tightening, legs bending as they readied themselves to spring ...

Then the telephone rang and brought him sharply back. He opened his eyes and looked at himself. A lynx with crutches?

He trudged over to the telephone and, in moments, requests to fill new orders were being printed out on the data transmission.

5 A wind rose in the night from somewhere downhill. It rolled past the houses of people sleeping, past empty factories and mills, past the chemical plant disturbing some still hovering fumes, and into Colin's yard where it picked up and dropped loose papers and trash. It came in through his window and the leaves of his fern trembled.

It brushed by Colin disturbing his sleep, and he shivered and rolled over. It hesitated, then it went on, out the other window to the pen of the sleeping seal.

She awoke, her senses alert. She turned her head trying to locate something within that wind.

The city's roar was distant and somewhat quieter at night, but there was a sound yet softer, yet more distant. Then it grew louder, a singing of a secret note. It became insistent, demanding, and finally inexorable as it pulled at her, commanding her deepest instincts.

She tried to crawl up out of her pen, her sharp black nails digging deep into the wood, but the wall was too high. She attacked the door next, bumping it at first, and then throwing her whole weight upon it, time after time, until some bolts loosened and the door gave slightly. The opening was still only half her width, but her loosely hung body was amazingly elastic, and as she pushed at the opening with all her strength her body bent and squeezed until it wriggled through.

Then, resting only a moment, she began her trek. Stretching herself full length on her stomach, she pulled herself forward by her front flippers, drew her body up, then stretched herself forward again like a holy man crawling on a penitential pilgrimage.

She limped past Colin's quarters and then past the chemical plant itself. Her movements became a pattern. She would pull herself three times then rest a moment. Three more times, then rest, an inchworm on an odyssey. Past the rancid river lined with chemical plants, over numerous rail spurs and rusting auto hulks, until she left the city far behind. Finally she inhaled a new smell and heard a new sound.

She climbed a final rock and saw it below, the seascape lit by the full moon, the water clean and pure. It washed in white foam over bizarre rock formations and threw itself against sheer cliff walls, then receded leaving momentary moonlight in stone and sand.

The wind carried whiffs of the sea to her on top of the cliff. Totally possessed, she climbed down a cliffside path, sliding with rocks and gravel in miniature landslides, scraping her skin and leaving smears of blood on the stones.

She crawled toward the smoothly breaking waves, digging out a strange pattern of a swirling where her rear flippers were dragged from side to side.

Finally she reached the wet sand and rested. The surf came in and she let it roll over her, washing away garbage, glass and gravel, soothing the wounds. She twisted about in the small puddles.

A second wave came in, lifting her. She swam with it and let it carry her out to sea.

Then she was gone.

6 Colin stood contemplating the trail in the sand, the wide swirling groove, the dried blood turning brown, all ending at the water's edge. Then he looked baffled out at the ocean.

For days afterward he did his work listlessly and mechanically, frequently letting the telephone ring on unanswered, reading numerous books and not absorbing a word.

He would set out the plates of food for the cats and dogs of the neighborhood again. He made no move to befriend them, merely watching quietly as they carried the bones back to their lairs. He would stand alone in the yard a long while, and finally look at the seal's empty pen, the metal rusting, the wood weathered and rotting.

Why did she leave?

He searched the books on seals. The folklorists spoke of the mysterious call of the sea, the zoologists of the seal's constant seeking of a downhill direction until it led to water, but of the source of that lure, the nature of its power, they had no answer.

Perhaps the answer was on too great a scale for mere books; it took something as vast as the Hall of the Sea in the city's museum.

He stood before a huge globe of Earth rotating slowly beneath a spotlight representing the sun. For a moment Colin felt he was drifting over the planet, watching as some astral spirit might, with the mountains of Europe and Africa raised in bold relief, their shadows shortening and lengthening dramatically as they came under the sun and then passed into darkness.

But then he saw what no space wanderer would have seen, the basin of the Atlantic sunk in similar relief as if drained of all its water. The greatest mountain range on earth is buried in that ocean, twisting from nearly North Pole to South Pole, a great central boundary line between Old World and New. Yet it ranges much farther, a full forty thousand miles in all. In its center, the Mid-Atlantic Ridge, the mountains extend for miles upward from the ocean floor. At times their tops break through the surface to become islands. The Azores sit on mountains nearly five miles high.

A deep gash cuts down the center of the Ridge, neatly midway between the continents, following their outline, the open wound where they split apart and drifted to their separate hemispheres.

The planet is fluid, lands still drifting, the shell still shrinking, leaving wrinkles like a drying apple, except that these wrinkles are great miles-high mountains.

The globe continued its rotation, carrying the Americans past Colin's vantagepoint and bringing the Pacific basin into view, an immensity greater than all the lands combined.

Fractures run laterally through the bottom as if scratched by some giant talons, and then many mountains break through the surface to become island chains—the Hawaiian Islands, the Gilbert, Marshall, Midway, Solomon.

Then Colin saw the most tortured area on earth. Here the work of the planet is still undone. A great ring of trenches encircles the Pacific basin and forms the "Ring of Fire," countless volcanoes, endlessly seething, around which occur four out of five of all earthquakes. The world is young here, still being born, the forces of creation still in evidence. The earth buckles and folds, pushing aside mantle to form deep trenches, wounds, and gashes, festering sores in the planet's skin. The deepest of these is the Marianas trench, seven full miles.

At a distance, the planet seems misnamed Earth for the continents are little more than floating islands in a great world sea that circles fully seven-tenths of the globe.

Suddenly Colin's world on land seemed limited.

In a glass case running the length of a corridor many fish were mounted and identified. A sign indicated that many times more still swam undiscovered in the sea, and scientists had deduced that eight-tenths of all life lives there.

Colin wondered why. He was already wondering if his seal knew something he didn't know.

Then he caught sight of an immensity hanging from the ceiling. A blue whale, the largest creature that ever lived, dwarfed Colin into an insignificant insect. It weighed two thousand times as much as he. At rest it was three stories high, and when diving, eleven stories. Its size was monstrous, yet its form exquisite, frozen in grand curves and sweeps as it swam in an imagined sea. It seemed more crippled than Colin or his seal, with no legs at all, yet it was more graceful than any bounding lynx or flying bird.

But in its skeleton lay two strange small bones, separated from the spine and quite without use, in the evolutionary process of disappearing completely. They were vestigial legs. This creature now so totally of the sea once walked the earth.

The flippers were once forelimbs and its bones still showed wrist and fingers. Its once pointed tail had broadened to a wide horizontal fluke for a propeller.

The sign asked:

> *What did this creature look like when it lived on land? No one knows, nor can anyone say for certain why it returned to the sea. Perhaps its legs were not strong enough to support its huge bulk and it sought the rest and buoyancy of the swamps.*

Colin looked down at his own legs, rubbed them in pain, and wondered. He read further:

> *The whale returned to the sea one hundred million years ago, and was eventually followed by other mammals. The longer they have been in the sea, the more adapted they have become.*
>
> *One can follow the path of that counterrevolution, the line circling back on itself, through the several sea mammals. The process begins with the sea otter, its hind paws webbed after two million years. Then the sea lion, all four limbs reverting to flippers. Then the seal, the*

*hind flippers dropping back to the tail. Then the mana-
tee, those hind limbs receding completely. And after a
hundred million years there is the whale, its foreflippers
short and stubby, powerful flukes like tail fins, the most
streamlined and free of the sea mammals.*

*But the circle is not yet closed. Even the whale con-
tinues evolving toward that goal, the ultimate return to
its birthplace.*

The information stirred something within Colin, some
elusive words, " 'I will go back to the sea' . . . Something
'sea' . . ."

There was an exhibit of embryos in bottles, varying species of mammals retracing their evolution in the womb.

They were all alike once. At the beginning seal resembled man. Both were sea creatures, with barely developed
limbs that were more like flippers, heads joined to bodies
without intervening necks, ears more like gills.

Then, as the embryos showed, their common ancestor
crawled onto land, the flippers became miniature claws.

But here the embryos diverged. Here they went separate
ways, for the seal embryo regrew its flippers while the human dveloped its limbs into hands and feet.

Yet, paradoxically, the human is still a sea creature. The
amniotic fluid in which his embryo floats is a miniature sea,
of the same saltiness as the sea of his aquatic ancestor.
When born, he will carry that same saline sea in his blood,
its minerals in his bones. His tears are the sea in his eyes,
sweat the sea on his skin. For all his life he will watch the
rolling waves of the sea with strange emotions he cannot
fathom.

Colin began to feel those emotions now, a yearning to
share the deep rest of the embryo, of the seal, of the whale
when it sought the swamps, to be cradled in the sea,
weightless and buoyant, rocked in the gentle waves.

". . . My mother, the Sea . . ." He remembered a poem
long forgotten, read in passing. Now he returned to his
room to search for it.

It was buried beneath texts of engineering and math-
ematics but at last he found the volume, its binding torn,
pages yellowed; the poem was "The Triumph of Time" by
Swinburne.

The verses gave words to his thoughts, spoke to his longing . . .

> *I will go back to the great sweet mother,*
>   *Mother and lover of men, the sea.*
> *I will go down to her, I and none other,*
>   *Close with her, kiss her, and mix her with me;*
>   *Cling to her, strive with her, hold her fast;*
> *O fair white mother, in days long past*
> *Born without sister, born without brother,*
>   *Set free my soul as thy soul is free.*

He returned to the place where the seal had entered the waves.

He closed his eyes, tried to forget the land, his loneliness, his pain, tried to imagine himself set free as the seal, as the whale.

> *Set free my soul as thy soul is free.*

But there was no vision, no release. When he opened his eyes, the hard earth still lay beneath his pained legs.

He looked out across the ocean. It was too late, far too late. He was old, humanity was old, the sea was old, magic was old.

He turned and hobbled away.

7 He floated buoyantly, cradled in the sea, rocked gently
in the waves. He was an embryo in his mother's womb
and his mother was the sea itself. All weight was gone,
all pain was gone, and there was only the deepest of rests.
There was a singing, a sweet and beautiful sound, a lullaby
. . .

He wakened out of his dream. He was in his bed in his
room. His body was heavy, his legs crippled. Glumly he listened to the sounds of night traffic coming in through his
window. There was no other sound.

He took the poem with him up the steps to his work
and read that first verse again and again.

> O fair white mother, in days long past
> Born without sister, born without brother,
> Set free my soul as thy . . .

The telephone interrupted, the office calling with new orders to fill. He adjusted the machines accordingly, and outside the pipes spewed more thick liquids into the river.

He stood on the shore where she had vanished before,
but now she reappeared far off, silhouetted in the glow of
the waters. She was the child of the sea and she called to
him in a voice almost unbearably lovely, singing to him to
join her. The song pulled at him, drew him nearer . . .
This time when he awoke, he heard another sound

through the city's roar, a lonely weeping, or a singing that was almost human.

He listened, trembling.

Finally he sat up, snapped on the light, and the sound was gone.

> *As for the Meremaids, it is no fabulous tale that goeth of them: for looke how painters draw them, so they are indeed: only their bodie is rough and skaled all over, even in those parts wherein they resemble a woman. For such a Meremaid was seene and beheld plainely upon a coast neere to the shore: and the inhabitants dwelling neere heard it a farre off to make a piteous mone, crying and chattering very heavily.*

So wrote Pliny the Elder in the first century.

> *This evening (June 15) one of our company, looking overboard, saw a mermaid looking earnestly upon the men. Her skin very white and long hair hanging down behind, of color black. In her going down they saw her tail, which was like the tail of a porpoise, speckled like a mackerel . . .*

So went the official log of Henry Hudson.

They were much seen in those days, dutifully and even casually entered in ships' logs.

Colin read on, dreamed and wondered, and again the telephone interrupted with its own rude song.

He lay cradled in the sea, gently rocked. At first he dared not open his eyes for he knew the dream would vanish, but the song called to him, imploring, until finally he dared look. Above him the ceiling of the sea shimmered in glorious colors. The song called to him and at first he dared not answer, knowing his body would buckle beneath him and drag him down.

Then, tentatively he moved his hands and feet and he suddenly felt like a feather caught in a gust of wind, so light he could dance if he wished, even fly if he would only

...

A metallic scream ripped through the waters, seared the colors to ash, wrenched him back to his bed and the pain.

He sat up. Outside a truck clattered and roared down the elevated highway.

"There are no sirens, no mermaids, no half-man half-fish, no human children of the sea. There are only wishful fantasies, fevered imaginations, dark superstitions ...

"Picture the sailor fearfully venturing out into unknown waters. He had known the land, but that was a mere fourth of the vastness and void of the sea. Strange clouds and fantastic shapes would hover over the horizon that stretched out into infinity. Entire islands would suddenly appear in the distance, and disappear as he approached. Or he might sail through an unending fog, a gray curtain cutting him off from any real world, and suddenly a giant bird might fly out of nowhere, travel through his world, and disappear into nowhere. The sea might turn brick red about him, as if it were bleeding. It is a time when to the ignorant all magic is possible.

"Now he hears something, a mournful voice, vaguely—but only vaguely—human, hoarse, unappealing, but he is six months out of port.

"Now a manatee or dugong appears in the water, seemingly standing upright, and she holds an infant to her breast with one flipper in a most human fashion. As the ship approaches, she plunges beneath the surface, flicking her tail in the air.

"Or the more sleekly shaped seal is spotted on a distant rock, basking in the sun. She has amazingly mobile flippers and scratches her forehead, or brushes her nose with the back of a hand. So the sailor believes and perhaps gives chase, much to his grief for he likely wrecks his wooden boat on uncharted rocks. If he survives, he will have stories to tell on his next voyage, and the others will be even more ready to believe.

"But today we cross a thoroughly charted sea to the roar of heavy diesels and hear no songs. We know of optical illusions and microscopic plants that discolor the water. We are no longer superstitious. We know better."

Colin sadly snapped the book shut as again the telephone rang.

She wore a cloak of corals and pearls that caught and held the fire of the sea. Green hair draped her exquisite head. When she called, this time he did not hesitate. He followed her into the water as she drew back, all the while beckoning him on. Finally he dropped his crutches, spread his hands to fly. How easy it was. He joined hands with her and they flew together, to her kingdom under the sea where her palace was made of corals and pearls that glowed from where the sun went at night, and the fish shone with that radiance.

Then it began to fade, and he felt himself pulled up and back, his legs growing heavier. Again she called to him, but he could not answer. He wanted desperately to remain, but the force pulled him back and yet further back until all was darkness and he opened his eyes and saw he was again on his bed in his room and his legs still hurt.

Then he listened. He could still hear that singing, echoing as if from some distant cavern. He reached for his crutches, and the singing faded.

With a sigh he let his crutches drop and he fell back on his bed. He lay there a good while, unable to sleep.

Finally he decided.

He drew himself out of his room, past the rancid river lined with chemical plants, over numerous rail spurs and rusting auto hulks until he left the city far behind. Soon a new smell and a new sound reached him. Climbing a final rock he saw the clean surf rolling over bizarre boulders and against sheer cliff walls, surfeited with mist, all catching the cold colors of the predawn sky.

Finally reaching the cool sand, he dropped his crutches and lay there, letting the water roll over him.

The tip of the sun rose just above the horizon, casting a gold spear across the sea. The clouds above colored the water with reds, yellows, and blues that intermingled with the blue-green of the water like a painter's palette. The waters beyond the rocks were smooth and calm.

Then he heard it in the distance, not quite a cry for it had melody, at once ancient and modal, and yet timeless. It echoed in some half-flooded cavern or between the steep walls of a cove.

He had read of that song and the singer. She sang in ages past to all people who lived by the sea, but never this age, this people.

But now Colin heard it as the Greeks heard it. They called her the Siren and pictured her face human, her body a bird, for they thought only birds could sing so sweetly. They thought she dwelt with her sisters on a lonely island where passing mariners were drawn by that singing.

As the centuries passed, her song was given to the voiceless sea nymph, called now the mermaid who sought the soul of a man to give and receive love. For love, she took off her precious skin so she might assume human form, gave up her fish tail for legs so that when she walked the pain would be as if she were walking on swords.

She sang as the Lorelei on the Rhine River, the Ningyo in Japan, the Melusine in France, the Morgan in Wales, the Rysalka in Russia, but in this age and time she was silent and unseen.

Yet now Colin stood by the shore and heard her.

He cupped his hand to his mouth and called. Soon he was caught up in it. The yelling seemed to release him, set free some long bound-up part of himself, and he yelled again and again.

It echoed off the distant rocks, and then far out in the smooth morning waters a gleaming apparition surfaced, silhouetted in the reddish gold light. Slowly, strongly, it began to grow, rising from the depths.

It was the child of the sea returning. Green hair draped her exquisite head. Her body was cloaked in fiery corals and pearls from her palace in the sea, where she danced to endless song. All this she was now giving up for a human soul, for love. She would take off her skin and walk with him on land, though each step would be as if she were walking on swords.

She approached the shore and crawled up on the sand.

She had grown considerably larger since he had seen her last, almost as big as he. Her baby fur had long since been shed, replaced by a sleek speckled gray coat glistening with wetness and decked with numerous barnacles and shells. Her once overlarge head now seemed exquisitely sleek in proportion to her full-grown body and was crowned with green seaweed. Her nostrils opened and closed with assurance.

He knelt so that he was eye to eye with her. Her large brown eyes had lost all trace of infancy and were now soft and calm, yet to Colin they held hint of great mysteries, of the depths in which she had swum, of secrets known only to children of the sea.

He touched her gray head, scratched her neck, rubbed the little holes that were her ears. She purred softly and touched her nose to his.

Suddenly he could restrain himself no longer and threw his arms about her. Then they rolled in the sand and played together until the sun rose high.

The tide slowly withdrew and the sand dried and whitened beneath them, wrapping them in a warmth beneath a warming sun. They lay together a long while without a motion or thought beyond this beach and this moment.

What would it be like to waken in her world?

Water had filled his limbs, his skin, his lungs. It tormented him, deformed him, and nearly killed him.

Did it now offer him rebirth?

8 What was this substance he feared so and yet now attracted him, that was the most common on earth and yet its rarest wonder, the agent of his near destruction and possibly now of new life?

He had in the past dealt with countless fluids, gases, and metals, analyzing their natures until their mysteries were revealed, and none had so strained his sensibilities, had eluded or baffled his intelligence as did simple common water.

He began as he usually did, by assembling all that was already known, except that now his research ranged from the present science to the ancient wisdom. Strangely, time after time there was a linkage between chemist and alchemist, between textbook and Holy Book. There was paradox upon paradox and miracle upon miracle.

Mere water.

Every drop of water now existing has always existed since Earth began, changing no more than its shape to steam or ice, but remaining the same molecule, the same water.

So said the textbook, and the Holy Book agreed. In the beginning, "... the Earth was without form, and void ... And the Spirit of God moved upon the face of the waters." The waters were in existence before Creation, before heaven and earth. The chaos itself was water.

Colin the chemist knew that life grew out of water, is dependent upon water, contains water in its being. Now he read of the mystics who knew this before the scientist.

The Spirit of God that moved upon the water also breathed life into Man, and so the spirit was the substance of life. So said the Bible, and so said other ancient peoples. They gave the sea different names and guises, Nephe and Naimu, Ea and Oannes, pictured her sometimes god sometimes goddess, but always the bringer of birth and the sustainer of life.

The sea created, but it also destroyed. An angered God crushed His creation in a great flood, returning the earth to water, to chaos. And so, interestingly, did those other far-flung gods. The bringer of birth and of death, and perhaps of both, of new life in death. With baptism, in those waters in which Colin was immersed as an infant, his old self had died, the old life of sin, and he had been born anew, a child washed pure and brought to eternal life.

Which would it do to him, restore him or destroy him? Did the books offer warning as well as wisdom?

Other books told him of this supernatural duality, how to magicians and priests it was the most powerful source of magic, black and white. Which spell would it cast for him?

By shore or river one could hear its voice, thundering or murmuring. One could look and see strange shimmerings on its face. Those who could understand its voice or read its images partook of wisdom accumulated since before Creation. And could Colin do so?

He came often now to the shore, to stare at its changing colors from dusk to dawn, to listen to its sounds in differing weather. He looked and listened intently, but the shimmerings and thunderings held their secrets to themselves.

He yearned for the wisdom denied him as he turned from ancient texts to modern and was soon as bewildered as others before him at this substance that obeyed no laws but its own, collecting endless paradoxes, and sustaining life within them.

Colin had always known, accepted as fundamental law, that matter contracted as it cooled. But water does not. A few degrees above freezing it expands, making the solid lighter than the liquid. Ice, then, floats atop the sea, protecting the life beneath from colder air. Also, free waters rise and fall with their changing temperatures, constantly refreshing and replenishing both depths and surface. Otherwise, the ocean would freeze from the bottom up and would soon be still and lifeless—as eventually would the whole planet.

Another paradox. It absorbs heat faster than any substance known—which was why Colin used it to cool the factory—and yet retains the heat longer, which was how that heated water could warm the entire building economically. So the oceans modify the extremes of temperature around the world, taking heat from the hot places quickly, retaining it until it can be given slowly to the cold places, keeping the temperatures of the planet within that very narrow band in which life can exist.

It is the impossible substance, the dream of alchemists, the universal solvent. Small rivers will carve canyons through the hardest rock. Even so-called pure or distilled water cannot remain in any container for long without eventually carrying off its chemical traces. Since it passes around the earth in its gaseous form and returns again as a liquid, it carries all the substances it touches. An isolated drop is a miniature complex of them all, and surely the most complex on earth. It carries all the various chemicals that make up all organisms and is therefore the essence of life, the vessel of the Spirit of God in which life is born and new life is given.

It is the only substance on the planet to exist in all three states simultaneously, and so partakes of the trinity of matter: air, earth, and sea; gas, solid, liquid; breath, flesh, blood.

Mere water.

The ultimate paradox. This, the very stuff of life, the mother of man and all living things, had now become a more hostile home for him than would the vacuum of outer space. Did she still rankle at Colin's ancient ancestor who turned his back on the sea some three hundred millions years ago? Certainly she did not welcome back men before Colin. For thousands of years they had dreamt of returning, of finding the freedom of a fish. Just beneath the surface a man could breathe with a simple straw, but as he went deeper and tried for greater liberation from the land, his equipment grew more complex until the self-contained breathing apparatus became an intricacy of regulators, valves, tanks, gauges, insulators.

Yet creatures before man had returned and found freedom there. The sea had seemingly welcomed back the whale, the manatee, the seal . . .

Colin met her often at the surf. One such time she came ashore and tried to pull him into the sea as so long before she had tried to pull him into a tankful of water.

Would it be so difficult?

As he saw the waves coming closer, he dug his crutches in the sand to brace himself, and drew back. He was a man, not a seal, and the sea could destroy him.

And yet . . .

Why not learn from the seal, from a teacher who had had herself millions of years to learn?

The water that absorbed heat so rapidly—thirty times faster than air—would carry off his own body heat. It would weaken and soon destroy him in the deeper waters. Why not her?

She had developed two distinct layers of fur with bubbles of air trapped between them, keeping her as well-insulated as a vacuum flask. Colin would translate her anatomy to his mechanics, changing fur to rubber, and air bubbles to latex foam.

In deep dives she conserved heat further by constricting her blood vessels, allowing just enough blood to flow to keep the cells nourished and prevent their freezing. Colin would translate this too, using the device of water pressure to constrict his extremities and slow the circulation on deep dives.

Her nostrils opened to receive air but closed tight as a drum when she dived. Colin would add a valve to his mask that would flip open to receive surface air but close shut when he dived.

Instincts and reflexes were much more elusive to duplicate. What for her were tiny nerves and cells became for him an intricacy of circuitry and sensors, such as the gauges and regulators to tell him when air was low.

But even the complexities of the diving gear were simple compared to those of the sea-home in which he hoped to live completely free of the surface. Here he would have to contend with metals and alloys, systems for navigation, ballast, pressure, electricity, air regeneration, water purification, and on and on. And where was the power to come from for them all?

The more independent he wished to be, the more complex the systems, the greater the power required. To be totally free of the surface and land called for an infinitely complex machine, therefore an infinitely large craft to house it and infinite power to propel and maintain it.

It was impossible, fundamentally impossible. Colin's computer would blow out its circuits in frustration. As did Colin.

But the seal had no such agonies. The sea itself was her sea-home, the waves her engine. Though they carried the power of winds thousands of miles away, yet they were her playthings. She would catch the curl and ride it as it propelled her faster than any bird, then break the surface, corkscrew in the air like a salmon before diving again, adding her own designs to its designs. She mocked Colin and his books, metals, machines, computers.

Who was he, this end product of evolution? How dare he turn his back on three hundred million years that it took to bring him up from the swamps? What arrogance. What stupidity.

It took no less than a conqueror of empires and all lands, Alexander the Great, to attempt the first conquest of the sea. He was said to have descended in a large glass urn and seen many wonders below, including giant crab fish, men with six hands, and a sea monster that took three days and nights to pass by. Even Alexander was humbled by this new empire.

And was Colin greater? Or was he merely a helpless gnome?

He laughed at his absurdity.

The sea glowed with a strange luminescence from the sun that lit its depths. She was returning to her kingdom and singing to him to join her. Her song was of almost unbearable beauty and it told of the freedom of the sea. It drew him to her, and she moved back keeping the distance.

He called to her but she would not wait.

The water grew deeper, crept up his scarred skin and

crippled legs, but caressed and soothed them. Already he was feeling those first signs of liberation. He went deeper, and yet deeper.

She plunged and glided like some great bird. How easy it must be. All he need do was throw off his crutches and give himself to her, to the sea.

He spread his hands, dropped down to the waves, let them take him, hold him, give him their freedom.

Suddenly the singing stopped and the light vanished. It was a vast abyss, a great blackness with no sign there was ever light in the universe at all, only darkness to its very edges, since the beginning of the world and for all time. It was a black quicksand pulling him down to lifeless depths with not a sliver of light or land to grasp.

Corrosive water tore at his skin. It reached into pockets and crevices in his bones and joints, shredded membranes, pulled tendons apart, sent splinters of bone flying into muscles like thousands of spears.

He tried to cry out, but the water reached for his lungs, crushed out millions of tiny cells.

... drowning ...

His heart grew irregular, beat wildly, wandered.

His body, his universe of billions of cells, screamed together for precious air. The scream gathered force, called on him. With some last tiny bit of strength from some dying source, the scream found voice ...

He sat up in bed perspiring, shivering, his heart pounding. Disoriented, he looked about until he saw in the dimness that he was indeed in his own place, books still lying in a heap on the floor.

He listened for the sound of surf or that voice, but there was only the dim roar of the traffic at night.

Restless, unable to sleep now, he reached for the books.

He read of the giant squid, eight powerful arms and two tentacles, together measuring seventy-five feet, and of one a century ago that attacked a full-sized schooner, wrapping its arms around the deck and high up the masts, pulling them down and vanishing with its wooden prey in a matter of minutes.

One squid was never seen, but the scars it left in battle

with a sperm whale indicated a creature two hundred fifty feet long. The sea was a place for warring giants.

There were legends of the Kappa, slimy green gremlins who came out of the sea to cut boats adrift, entangle propellers, or even jump aboard at night to wreak general havoc. There was a hierarchy of the Dragon Kings, from the smallest the size of a caterpillar, to the Great Dragon as great as the sea itself.

Whales battered ships, sea serpents came ashore to devour cattle and humans and even seaweed came to life and strangled helpless sailors.

Which was fact and which fancy? They intermingled easily, for the sea is the dark place and less is known of it than the moon.

If the mermaid, the Siren could exist, then why not these other nightmares?

Why not his own nightmare? He turned again to the books about her. From the time of the ancient Greeks there were warnings of the Siren songs, for the human bones of sailors and the remains of their ships were piled high on her island.

The mermaids were perverse in their contempt for men, even as some might love them. They danced with delight in the waters when a storm was approaching that would wreck ships, but in fair weather they were filled with despair and sank gloomily to the depths.

Even if one did fall in love with a mortal man, she might pull him to the sea and drown him rather than follow him to land.

The Church looked anew at the Greek tales. It saw the ship as the Church upon the seas of the world, the sailors as the Christian people, and to listen to her song on life's voyage meant either physical death, or moral death in yielding to seduction.

Colin reached for his crutches. They felt strong as he put his weight upon them; they would never crumble beneath him. He felt for the floor with his feet; it was firmly rooted and unwavering. He looked out the window. The city was dark except for the street lamps and the headlights of an occasional car or truck; there were no unexplained luminescences, no strange sounds.

He pulled himself out the door. The air was slightly tainted, but there was plenty of it, more than he could breathe, enough for all humanity.

He studied each familiar building, each landmark. It was his world, uncomplicated, uncluttered, unambiguous. Beyond lay water with its duality, to give either rebirth or destruction.

Beware the Siren song that pulls the ship off course on its voyage through life, for the sailor's bones will lie bleached on some far island, or in the depths, while she weeps false tears.

Even the pain as he dragged himself down to the beach gave him reassurance that he was alive, gave that life reality.

He waited for her by the beach.

She appeared first a silhouette against the soft dawn sky. She called to him in that same modal scale he now knew so well, but he did not answer.

She came close to shore and called again, and again he did not answer.

Finally she crawled on shore, wrapped her flippers around him, tugged with her teeth, tried to pull him toward the water.

"No! I'm not going with you." Now he pulled at her, but she wriggled out of his grasp and backed away to the waves.

"If you don't come with me now, it's goodbye. I've got my own world." He turned away and hobbled up the beach. He heard nothing. Only when he was at the top of the hill did he turn and look back.

She was frantic, hobbling up the hill after him, then turning back to the sea, then toward him again, and those false tears were rolling down her cheeks. Finally, she slumped and rested in the sand.

The waves rolled around her, washed the sand from her, lifted her gently and carried her away. As he looked he could see her form grow smaller and smaller, and then vanish as she dived into her home.

He looked at the empty sea a long, long while, then with tears of his own he dragged himself back to his own home.

9 The cats and dogs did not appear when he called. He called again, louder, and his voice bounced off a gas storage tank, across to the auto graveyard, and returned unavailing.

He went back to the zoo, looking for the lynx, then the snake, but the entire zoo was empty, quiet and lifeless except for the yellowed and dried newspapers blowing across the ground, lifting themselves into serpentine shapes and then dying.

The desolation matched his own.

On his way out Colin stopped before the seal pool. The weeds that had worked their way through the crumbling concrete had turned brown and shriveled. He stood there long moments. Then he returned home.

He turned from books to films, to little flickerings that told where she came from and the things that shaped her life.

She came from a great colony brimming with hundreds, thousands packed close on the ice. As Colin watched, he saw life in all its wondrous complexity unroll before him, and he lived it with them. It was contained in a square of light on a small white screen, but even so, Colin felt he could almost share that life.

The camera comes closer and the great colony is delineated into its members. Nearest the water are the bachelor males, most of them packed closely together, trying to sleep in the crush. The slightest movement of one, though, disturbs the whole crowd.

The camera moves on, to where the more fortunate and

49

aggressive males keep their harems. One old great bull circles his own, keeping a wary eye out for any intruders on his territory, while sniffing each female in turn, looking for signs of arousal for he must keep them continually satisfied.

Still, one cow wanders off, and with a loud snort the bull charges and shoves her forcibly back into the territory. As he does so another female wanders off on the opposite side, and with a more aggravated—and more tired—snort, he goes charging after her.

Suddenly he looks offscreen and clucks suspiciously. A young bachelor is approaching, at last deciding he has the strength to defeat the patriarch and take over the harem. Neighbor seals flee in all directions. The two bulls exchange chugging threats and some half-hearted lunges which grow fierce. The young bachelor is brought down with a slash across his flank. He hobbles off, bleeding, howling in pain. He must sustain many such scars before he can finally take a harem for himself. And then he too will be contending with a dozen wandering females whom he can only keep by constant bullying and continual battle with other younger aggressive bachelors.

The society of the seals seems loveless. It is based on rule by force, terror, and deceit. A human counterpart would be barbaric.

But love is being saved toward one end, and it becomes evident as a cow lies on her side, rocking back and forth until a little head protrudes from her womb, wrapped in a pink membrane, entering the world to its mother's contractions, advancing then retreating as if in alternate boldness and shyness until finally half its body is visible. Suddenly the membrane breaks, and the pup slides out onto the ice, wet and steaming, staring at the world with large brown eyes. The mother nuzzles her child, breathes in his odor, and howls a cry the pup imitates in his weaker wail. Thus by smell and sound the mother learns her child.

The wetness freezes into ice on the pup, and though he shivers for a short while the ice will actually protect him from the colder air. Finally when the pup sloughs off the ice, the fur beneath is no longer wet and begins to fluff out, soft, white, and thick.

The seal has two enemies, the polar bear and the killer

whale, who crave it for food. Its fur however has given it a third enemy, the most relentless and crafty of all. But of course the pup knows nothing of these dangers. He bawls hungrily until his mother with a final contraction pushes out a little black nipple. The pup suckles the richest milk of any mammal, and is soon bulging like a little fur ball while his mother strokes him affectionately with her flipper.

Up and down the ice the scene is repeated, each infant adding its own cry until there is a cacophony of fifty thousand howls and wails, all seemingly alike and yet each so subtly different that a mother will recognize the distinct musicality of her own child and will tolerate no intruders.

In that great crowded nursery there are inevitably some mix-ups, some pups trying to suckle from wrong teats, but the cows fling away the intruders, leaving them to wail helplessly, trying one mother after another until they find their own.

The bulls ignore the noise and sleep.

Then amidst these sounds there is an unaccountable distant bass, a rumbling felt through the ice rather than heard. The seals do not notice, except for one old bull who lifts his head and looks out through the mist, sees nothing, grunts, and settles back to sleep.

The rumbling grows louder as if the ice were trembling to a herd of approaching caribou. The bull does not warn his fellows but picks himself up and fearfully hunches toward the water, almost stepping on pups, terrifying other seals in his path.

Uncomprehending, they follow and the fear spreads outward in a ripple. Hundreds of seals scramble in the direction of the water, leaving the pups behind.

For these it is too late, for now strange specters upright on hind legs appear out of the mist.

More seals hobble toward the safety of the sea, but now the specters appear suddenly from all sides crying "Kar-kar-kar-kar-kar-kar," and beating metal upon metal in shattering din.

There is a loud crack and a bull falls, its huge mass collapsing in a hulk. A second crack and a cow drops. A third, a fourth, a fifth, and soon blood is flowing into the water or congealing on the ice. The rookery is by now a pandemonium of terrified barkings and howls, clanging metal, and the strange cries of the specters.

The pups crawl slowly and helplessly, unable to comprehend the commotion, and certainly unable to escape from it. One pup still tries to suckle the teat of its dead mother.

The specters come forward, crowding the remaining seals together. They wear heavy fur coats and boots. Their faces are masked in wool revealing only eyes and mouths, or smeared with insulating seal blood. They carry stout oak clubs and wander among the pups, by now frantically crawling atop each other.

Now the specters start swinging those heavy clubs on small frail skulls. An orphan hobbles with its eyes wide in fright, wailing a pitiable *maa*. A furred boot steps in front, blocking its path, and a club comes crashing down.

One pup draws her flippers close, pulls her head under her soft neck and makes no further move. Inside her darkness she feels warm and protected, shut out from the horror. From outside she seems a lifeless furry bolster, but the specter is not fooled. A club finds the life within that cushion and crushes it.

Another pup approaches the specter and wraps tiny flippers around the furred boot in affection, and wails for its milk. Instead the club comes down. Its cry is cut short, its flippers drop.

One mother fights for her child. She charges the specter, her bearlike teeth drawn in a snarl. The specter retreats, but another crack sounds from behind, and the mother collapses.

The tempo picks up. Left, right, left, right, on and on the specters go, cutting down the frantically wriggling pups on all sides like farmers wandering among waving wheat with scythes. And indeed, the euphemism given the carnage is the "seal harvest."

Far into the day the clubbing continues until fifty thousand pups lie dead, and now newly armed specters come onto the ice. These carry steel knives. They grab pups by the hind flippers, spin them over, puncture their throats and in swift strokes cut away pelts, flippers, and blubber.

The pregnant cows are flayed open and unborn infants pulled out of their wombs. These too are stripped and skinned. Livers are cut out and tied on belts for some gourmets. The penises of the adult males are sliced off, later to be ground up for aphrodisiacs.

The by-now bloodied specters work more feverishly for the sun is beginning to set, and soon the ice is a grotesque palette of blood, intestines, skinned carcasses.

The screen went white as the film ended. Colin sat paralysed with horror. Then he tore the reel off the projector and flung it across the room as if it itself were bloodied.

He pulled open the curtains, letting daylight flood the darkened room. Outside, smokestacks poured out their smoke and fumes. The exhaust from thousands of vehicles hung in a cloud over the city, filtering the sunlight into a strange pale-green overcast. The city was drowning in its own waste.

Well, let it. Let whatever happens to them go on and happen. He could no longer live among them, not at the edge of their world, nor in their world at all.

Whatever he was now, he was no longer human for he no longer wished to be.

I shall sleep, and move with the moving ships,
Change as the winds change, veer in the tide . . .

10 The puzzle remained. What source of power could he tap? How could he move underwater as the ancient ships sailed the surface? If he were only above the water instead of beneath it, the winds would be that source, as unending as the warming of the sun and the rotation of the earth.

Why not compromise then? Sail the surface with the wind, never coming ashore, living between two worlds? But to live between worlds is to live in neither.

Yet ... wind ... not only to sail by, but to power all his systems without waste, a perfectly closed system in which every bit of energy is pulled back in and re-used.

But he would be underwater, and there is no wind underwater.

Yet ... think a moment. Water and air are both fluids, and subject to the same laws. Both are warmed by the sun, spin with the earth and yet slip free of it. Just as warm air is lighter and rises, and its place is taken by cooler air at the bottom, so it must be with water. It *must* move as the wind moves.

Thoughts came excitedly tumbling one upon another.

The warm waters at the equator must go somewhere when they rise. Why not to the cold waters of the poles? One movement, longitudinal, equator to pole.

They must be spun round at the equator by the earth's rotation. A second movement, latitudinal.

That same rotation would spin the longitudinal waters in great circles. A third movement.

And like interlocking gears, they would spin countercurrents on either side . . . and beneath. It was getting immensely complicated, and he began to feel dizzy almost as if he himself were being spun in those directions, yet he knew these complexities would allow him to sail wherever he wished, at whatever depth.

The lands, continents, islands would deflect them, set them into new patterns, but could not stop them. Yet more complexities.

Charts. There had to be charts. Surely for the surface currents as they were used by sailors, but what of the deeper currents, the ones that ran within currents, and counter to the countercurrents?

He searched feverishly through his books and finally found them, sketchy, far from complete, but already complex, with arrows in curves and circles, varying directions, dimensions and velocities at differing depths, but eventually interweaving all the flowing waters of the world.

He could design a ship to sail within those currents, with steel fins for sails, navigating as surely as sea captains had for the centuries before him. For electric power a waterwheel could spin a generator, which would in turn power all the other needed systems. For food, the same as the other creatures of the sea.

He drew up sketch after sketch, refining the concept, drafting and redrafting specifications. The computer that worked the plant now worked for him, adjusting circuits, refining measurements, then feeding them to the machines which then cut, stamped, shaped and joined metals and glass in obedience.

Finally a craft emerged, and from his observation post Colin tended it carefully, had it cradled and conveyed to the waiting flatcar outside. As if working a toy train, he guided it from rail spur to river, and that night Colin boarded the plant's diesel-powered utility boat and towed his creation downriver, out to the harbor, then south to the clean waters. Here he was within sight of the cove where the seal entered the sea and where he would soon follow. He turned the proper valves, and the sea-home gave up its air reluctantly, with squeals and moans as the water came in and filled ballast tanks to proper levels.

As it drifted beneath the waves, it seemed like some living creature pulled down to the depths as Colin himself had floundered in black waters in his dreams. He peered through the waters hoping to see the craft settling, anchoring itself automatically above the sea-bed. But it was lost to sight too quickly. He could only hope.

For long moments he wondered if he were mad. Then, held there, he tried to look beyond, into the deepest of the depths searching for he knew not what. But there was nothing. Colin could neither read nor hear the sea's language. It held its secrets to itself.

A sudden chill. There was no one to make the journey with him. He would pass through the barrier to live alone if he succeeded, and die alone if he failed.

At last he turned the small boat and guided it to the beach. Here the high cliffs came up almost to the edge of the sea, blocking the sign of anything on the land above that might give clue of place or time.

A wind moaned down the canyon, sending a high surf rolling over jagged boulders and pounding against the cliff walls, slowly sculpting strange shapes into the seeming solid rock, building a beach a few grains at a time in one place, carrying it away a few grains at a time in another.

In human time it was totally desolate. There was no sign of civilization, or of humanity, nor indeed any indicator whether human beings had yet to appear on the planet, or had long since left it.

He thought of a girl he had not thought of in a long while. Had she thought of him?

He looked out across the water, cupped his hands to his mouth and gave a long wordless yell in that strange modal scale of his seal. The cry echoed off the cliffs and was swallowed up in the waves. He waited a good long while and called again, and again there was nothing. So even she had forgotten him.

At last he put on his diving gear and went out across the sand, hampered more than ever by the heavy tanks, blubbery suit, and rubber flippers.

Then he reached the detritus of the sea, the waste cast

up by the wind and waves. He came upon dried and whitened shells that crunched underfoot. His feet touched withered filmy bags, some with air pockets so they popped as he stepped on them. Dampish and foul-smelling straw caught at his legs, wrapped itself round and entangled him as he dragged his feet through. He passed amputated claws, bits of bones and rotting flesh. He gasped and nearly gagged, and went on with sweat rolling down inside his rubber skin.

Then the waves were washing about his feet and legs. The water did not soothe as in his dream, but stung with its iciness.

The water crept up around his body, and after a few more steps his crutches would no longer touch bottom.

Now he would close the valves on his mask and breathe from his tanks, but to do so he must take his hands from his crutches and let the water support him. He must cut himself off from both land and air, and give himself totally to this third element.

He let his crutches go gingerly, first the left, then the right. The planet dropped away beneath him and he was falling into a bottomless pit. The sea reached up to pull him down. Water came through the valves, into the mask, then down his throat reaching for his life.

He tried to cry out but only coughed and gagged, strangling in fluids as he heard his cells scream for bits of air.

He flailed in the water, grabbing on to it for a handhold, but it gave way between his fingers. At last the scream found passage and escaped, venting itself to the land and air, calling for help that would never come, and he knew he was dying alone.

Now something solid and floating, one of his crutches. He grasped it, then the second one, and soon he felt the solid ground beneath his feet. He worked the crutches back beneath his arms, then, struggling to keep his head above water, he made it back to the beach.

He did not feel safe until he was out of reach of the waves, and only then did he let himself drop to the warm dry sand, unbuckling the heavy gear to let it fall nearby.

He lay there shivering a long while as only one who came close to death shivers.

Finally he rolled on his back and looked about at his lonely surroundings. Behind him were high looming cliffs, with the city out of sight beyond. Above him was the morning sky. And ahead lay the open sea.

He did nothing more for a long while.

"Damn," he said finally.

11 There was no telling how long he lay on his back, for his mind was a total blank as he stared helplessly at an equally blank sky. At last he became aware of a subtle darkening in one corner and for a moment he blinked and squinted, thinking it was something in his eye. Then he realized the darkening was in the sky itself and he thought there was a fire somewhere nearby.

But the color was a grotesque olive-drab, quite unlike ordinary smoke. It was the oxides and sulfides of the city's waste.

The cloud was creeping south, tarnishing all natural and man-made things in its path, reaching for this hidden spot. Even as Colin watched, the bright sky was darkening to the pale-green overcast.

Instinctively he drew back, and looked out to the ocean. The waters were reaching for him again, the wash of each wave edging further up the beach.

With a shudder he dug his hands into the sand and pushed his way farther up until suddenly his back touched the rocks. Here he was trapped, able only to watch each foaming wave's subtle advance on the land, while above him the haze encroached on the sky.

The sun crept low near the horizon, lengthening the shadows beneath the wind-swept dunes, making them craters in some lunar landscape. Breaking across them were his own tracks, also made bolder by the setting sun, and even less real. For a while a passerby might wonder at the tiny but deep holes made by his crutches, the swirlings of his flippered feet as they dragged behind, flat and useless. But soon the sea would wash over them, the beach made again a trackless void, that solitary life gone and forgotten.

Of course there would still be the tracks of the elements, the mounds swept together by eddies of wind, the smaller ripples formed by the backwash of waves, the miniature canyons carved by rivulets returning to the sea. But these were all.

And yet . . .

As the sun went lower it brought out other subtler markings explainable by no force of elements. These were small and shallow, almost not there at all, as if made by ghostly fingers.

Here, a straight but quivering V-shaped groove. Crossing it, an imprint of miniature rails and ties. Further on, dozens of elfin holes, and tiny piles of dirt at the mouth of each to indicate the burrowers were still inside.

Colin was not alone.

But what kind of creatures were they? He poked his finger through one hole and felt a stirring beneath. He pulled away fingerfuls of sand but the frightened creature burrowed deeper. He tore away a handful, but saw only the sandy wake of an animal digging yet deeper.

He stared at the other holes, the homes of dozens of tiny burrowers that made their homes under his feet, at the other varied tracks that terminated in little mounds or depressions, all in the path of the inexorably rising tide.

Soon water would sweep across and engulf them in what would be a cataclysm on their scale, softening then disintegrating their homes, carrying them out to sea, letting them die screaming if such little creatures could scream.

Even now the water crept up rock walls cutting the route by which Colin had come and by which he might have escaped. The beach that was open a few hours before was now an enclosed cove, surrounded by high ledges jutting into deep water.

The waves washed over his own tracks, filling in the holes, flattening the mounds, and easily obliterating the other nearby tiny tracks. Then the water touched his feet, shocking him with its coldness. Still he did not move, held fixed by the sight of the coming catastrophe.

The water retreated, leaving the sand smooth and gleaming with the orange colors of the late afternoon sun. For a moment Colin thought this the apex of the tide, that the hidden creatures had cleverly calculated that point and safely built their homes beyond.

But now the waves came in again, just that bit further, crossing that margin and rushing down hundreds of holes, chasing after the creatures far faster than they could burrow. The sands shifted, the water bubbled up from the holes, and then suddenly the beach came alive with hundreds of creatures rising out of the mud, taking from the water whatever it had to give, then sinking back as the wave washed over them again.

Now as the water retreated some of the mites went tumbling after, reaching for it even as it reached again for them, burrowing just deep enough to avoid being swept away, sticking up little feathery appendages to grab food and moisture into microscopic mouths.

About Colin on the beach lived a myriad of creatures, burrowing, hopping, cemented to rock, but tied equally to land and sea, living in the rhythms of the tides, sweeping in nutrients with tiny arms or sieves or siphons, enough to sustain them the half-day till the waves reached for them again. With each incoming tide, a dead beach was reborn.

> *My lips will feast on the foam of thy lips,*
> *I shall rise with thy rising, with thee*
>   *subside . . .*

He went out on the ledge and looked down at the glaring surface of deep water. It was more than a mirror reflecting the sky and his own image, or the simple interface between elements. It was a physical force quivering with its own strength, a barrier against the spent sky and sterile land, keeping safe whatever lay below.

Those creatures of the beach that lived in their halfway world could slip beneath the barrier, infiltrate at the edges, but he, the man who would return completely into its depths, could do so only by throwing himself against it body and spirit, risking death and entrusting it to bring him . . . what?

Again he felt that chill of loneliness, and one last time

he cupped his hands to his mouth and called out for her in the notes of her song. Again there was no answer, no gray silhouette dancing in the waves or seemingly standing upright in deep water. There was only the quivering glass beneath.

One must be born alone and die alone.

He cast a final look about at the cliffs, the overhanging haze, and the city beyond. There was nothing further for him here. He closed the mask, released his crutches, and gave himself totally to the sea.

He was falling toward that glass and suddenly it seemed he would be crushed against it. He shrieked, tried to turn time backward, but it was too late. His body slammed against the glass and it splintered into a thousand pieces, each shard piercing his skin and bones. Suddenly he was immersed in it, suffocating, trying to gain a handhold on glass that melted at his touch.

He thrashed wildly to keep his head above the surface, but he was sinking, strangling, dying. It was no dream.

A big form bumped his faceplate. Terror-stricken he turned and saw two black holes peering at him through the mask. He grabbed at the creature for support, felt a soft furred body quiver with effort, and flippers gyrate as an animal struggled and pulled him up to the surface.

They broke into the sun together, and he saw she had not forgotten him.

Her nostrils opened and she took a couple of deep breaths. He had designed his gear to imitate her, and he imitated her now, opening the valves on his mask and taking desperate gulps of air.

She supported him instinctively, the same instinct with which her kind supported their infants until they learned the control.

As Colin found he could breathe, his panic gradually subsided. Soon he relaxed enough to close his valves and cautiously breathe his bottled air. He would not drown, and his breathing became regular and natural. He let go of her and was astonished to find himself floating, bobbing comfortably in the waves as he had seen her do.

He turned to watch her descend slowly as she did that

first time in the tank. He wanted to follow but hung clumsily on the surface, unable to sink.

He watched her. She exhaled bubbles as she descended, controlling her buoyancy by the amount of air in her lungs. He did the same, expelling most of the air in his lungs and breathing with the air remaining.

He began to sink, for the first time feeling liberation from the weight of his body. He kept his breathing shallow, and felt less grating pain with less expanded lungs.

He felt years drop away, memories returning of a time his body felt this light and free. He exulted in the sensation, not daring to open his eyes for fear it would all vanish and he would be back in his bed, his body again a prison.

Finally he looked.

Above him the sea's surface rose and fell in smooth rollings. The sunlight sifted down in long shafts, as in a Gothic cathedral. The wind stirred the surface and the sunlight shattered into explosions of color. Those long shafts of light were now bent through stained glass of every hue imaginable.

The sea gently rotated him so that his gaze followed those shafts of light to the bottom, now muted shades upon the ocean floor.

He imagined himself a bird flying high above some long-forgotten earth vista, for below him were tiny hills and valleys in spring bloom, with white and red blossoms among strangely misplaced tropical palm trees.

Then he was startled by another bird flying alongside. A common sea bass, flying in effortless motion with slight wriggles of its body and delicately fluttering fins. Its coat was a rustic olive-green with iridescent rainbows as its scales caught the light.

Then a school of jellyfish, not the dried-out filmy bags that washed ashore, but a ballet chorus in silken costumes banded in subtle pinks and pale blues. Their delicate, almost transparent tutus opened and closed as each kept separate time to its own unheard music.

Now a school of herring, row upon row in perfect military formation. They gave way for him, forming a great ripple that caught the sunlight, a gleam that traveled the length of the parade.

He descended deeper to the palm trees. Their fronds were more like leathery fringes banded in dark reds or rich browns, undulating in some undersea wind. He reached out to touch them, and in an instant the numerous fronds vanished into the tiny trunks.

His feet touched bottom, and a rock came alive beneath him, shaking sand off its back, and gracefully flapping speckled wings as it flew off.

It was the world of his dreams.

He was shocked out of it by a rude bump. Angrily he turned to see who had wrenched him from this trance and saw his seal swimming about him. He reached toward her, but she glided easily out of reach. He tried to swim after her, but when he brought his hands forward the water pushed him back. When his hands went up, he went down. When they went down, he went up. It was not like swimming on the surface, where he could swing his hands easily through air to then push against the denser water.

He felt terror return.

She bumped him again as if to admonish him, and circled about him as if to show how it should be done. Chagrined, he watched her. She swam by pushing with her rear flippers, bending them back and forth like sculling oars. He imitated her, bringing his legs up and down as she brought hers side to side. He spurted forward, but his dangling arms and tensed body set him into gyrations.

She bumped him again, and again he watched her. She was relaxed except for those particular working muscles. Imitating her, he let his body go limp, once more taking pleasure in its buoyancy, letting his trust grow.

Slowly, hesitantly, he again tried. Keeping his body relaxed, he lifted his legs and dropped them. To his surprise he shot cleanly ahead. Again he tried, up with his legs straight, down with his knees bent. Once more, up straight, down bent, and he was gliding in a smooth continuous motion. He continued imitating her, thrusting his hands out for stabilization.

She tilted her flippers left, and this allowed her to bank to the left. He watched, and followed.

She banked into a complete roll-over, and he found he could follow even then.

She skimmed the surface and jackknifed, her head down, her tail out of the water pointing straight up, and with one stroke of her flippers dove to the bottom.

He did the same, climbing to the surface thrusting his head down, his legs into the air, giving him added weight, and he found himself in an instant at the bottom.

She was waiting there for him.

Again he reached out to grab her and again she backed out of reach. He swam directly toward her, but she was gone. He looked about him, and suddenly got bumped from behind. He pumped his legs harder, tried to bank toward her, but could not turn that sharply and she was gone again.

She allowed him to grab her, but she constricted her elastic body and simply slid out of his grasp. Then she was below him, above him, thrusting herself between his legs and about his shoulders, under his arms and along his back, dancing circles about him, while he laughed in his exhilaration.

Colin wanted this to be his world forever, but now he saw it was not really his. His limits were measured by the air gauges which even now told him his time here was running out.

He sighed, and turned away from his seal to find the sea-home sunk nearby. So freedom was to be forever rationed, given out in dollops the size of his air tanks. No matter how far beneath the sea and into his new life he might venture, he was still a prisoner of his humanness, with no more than brief periods of parole.

But then as he came within sight of the craft his gloom lessened. After all, he was no prisoner. He could do as he wished. He need only open the hatch and enter, refill his tanks from the air regenerator and return to the sea at will.

No trouble, really.

12 For the first time he saw it as his home. It hung above him, awesome and frozen as if suspended from the ceiling of the sea, much like the great whale in the museum. At its tail were the steel flukes of the rudder assembly, and from there the body broadened sharply to contain the massive and complex systems needed to sustain Colin and guide the ship. At its widest point protruded seeming flippers, the metal sails to maneuver the ship in the currents.

The underbelly bulged with ballast tanks and batteries, the latter storing the power generated by the waterwheel which spun in the current flow like a miniature windmill.

The long solid trunk was welded to a comparatively small rounded head, the cabin, shaped in a sphere to withstand the deep-sea pressures. It was ringed with several eyes, portholes facing out in different directions.

The cabin had to be kept small in relation to the rest of the ship, but Colin had still managed to work in the needed instruments, a galley, bunk, and even his music collection. Warmth, light, and air awaited him inside, just the other side of the hatchway. That door was in the bottom of the hull so that it could be entered from the sea and still keep out water, much like an inverted glass.

Confidently, Colin swam up to the wheel and, gripping it firmly gave it a measured turn. It remained stuck.

Surprised, he pushed harder, but he only spun himself in the opposite direction.

What was wrong? The wheel he knew was balanced and geared to spin easily with a few pounds of pressure. A child could turn it.

In desperation, he pounded on the wheel, but the blow only sent him rocketing backward.

Then he realized. He was pushing with those few pounds and the wheel was resisting with that same force, action generating reaction pushing in the opposite direction, against and through him. He wouldn't have noticed it above with his heavy earthbound body to absorb it, but here he was neutrally buoyant. A few pounds of pressure was an infinite force to someone of no pounds at all. If the wheel turned with a featherweight of force he could never turn it.

On land, man under stress has been known to lift automobiles. He can be a superman, if the need arises, but underwater . . .

Colin took a deep breath and rose up, bumping the bottom of the sea-home. He exhaled, and descended back to the wheel. He thought a moment. Breathe in, ascend. Breathe out, descend. When he exhaled he was heavier. It was the air that was lightening him. He had to expel all the air possible from his lungs and tanks, and so approach death. That air suddenly became very precious in its rarity, far more so than a canteen of water in a desert, for suffocation killed more quickly than thirst.

Air more precious than water?

Had he chosen wrong, then? He looked at the glittering surface far above. There was plenty of air for the breathing, all he could ever want. Here below there were only the cupfuls in his tanks and lungs.

He could ascend to the surface, renounce the water and return, if the land would take him back. But he had to make that choice now. The pressure of the sea, the weight of all the water above him, had compressed all the air pockets in his body, in his lungs, his sinuses, his inner ears, even the cavities in his teeth.

If he ascended too quickly, faster than his rising bubbles, all the air pockets would expand too quickly, rupturing his ears and lungs, while the air dissolved in his blood would bubble out like soda in a suddenly uncapped bottle, and the bubbles would collect in his limbs leaving excruciating pain and paralysis.

The land would take him back, but on *its* terms, and it would punish him, cripple him many times over.

Choose! Now!

He opened his tanks, and the precious air escaped in great bubbles that rose freely to the surface as the water poured in. He opened the valves on his mask, and the water pushed in around his face. Then finally he gave up the most precious air of all, that in his lungs.

Now, straining, he tried to turn the wheel. It still did not budge. He heard a ringing in his ears and thought of those bubbles breaking free on the surface, their new liberty almost mocking him.

So he had chosen wrong and was going to die.

The last drops of air . . .

Expel even that last air.

He exerted his lungs to the limits of his strength and forced out every possible particle.

The ringing grew louder, blackness crept in at the edges of his vision.

Slowly the wheel turned, the hatch opened, and he rose up into air and life. He flipped open the valves and gratefully breathed the plentiful air of his sea-home, then abruptly started sinking back into the sea. Once again the water choked him as it entered his mouth and throat.

He had expected to rise up easily into the room, but there was no longer air in his tanks for buoyancy. He held on to the edge of the hatchway and tried to pull himself up but his tanks were awesomely heavy. Another moment of terror.

At last he unstrapped the tanks behind him, held them with one hand in the water where their weight was practically neutral, and with one supreme effort pulled himself up into the sea-home with his other hand. Once inside he tied the tanks to the nearest projecting ledge. He would have to recover them after he refilled them, so he crept like a wetted animal to the air pipe. The water followed and swirled around him as if refusing to let go. Once again he had to pull his mouth above its level.

Bewildered again, he pulled himself up by the handholds and stared down at the rising water. The inverted glass should have kept the interior completely dry . . . and then he remembered. Were that glass pushed deeper into the sea, the water would compress the air and squeeze its way in. Colin would have to increase the air pressure until it equaled the outside water pressure.

He opened the valves of the pressure system. More air hissed into the cubicle from the air regenerators, and gradually the water receded.

At last he could rest. He pulled himself across the room by handholds to the tape player, and put on the D major Horn Concerto, surely the most buoyant Mozart. Then, exhausted, he fell on his cot.

There was a real beginning, an operatic introduction for the French horn, the hunting horn of noble ancestry and bearing. It was an heroic beginning, and Colin heard his own reflection in it.

Yet the music suggested also the antics of the clown. Colin thought now of his own imbecility in trying to open the hatch.

Could he have foreseen the problem? He needed weight one moment, buoyancy the next. Obviously a paradox that demanded to be solved.

He began with one of the seal books.

Seals, when they wish to achieve negative buoyancy, or weight in water, will swallow stones which they disgorge when no longer needed.

Beneath his hero's mask lay a total fool, and Colin laughed loudly at himself.

He had no intention of swallowing stones, but the act suggested a belt with pockets for them, and he began designing one as the music played on.

Mozart's clown-hero was now a presence in the cabin and began to dance grinning all the while. It beckoned to Colin to follow. "Me? Really?" thought Colin, and the clown nodded. Colin's head grew light, then the lightness reached the rest of him, and now Colin danced and flew in the room as he had danced in the sea. It was exhilarating . . . and dizzying.

The clown came to the hatchway, with the water beneath glowing in a luminescent green circle, and with a laugh disappeared into the sea. The clown's song became the Siren's. The circle grew larger as Colin approached it until it reached out toward him, and suddenly he was inside it.

In the sea kingdom he knew he could breathe. He opened his lungs and inhaled glorious water ...

The scene vanished. He had insanely crawled to the hatchway and plunged his head into the sea. Now he was coughing with water in his lungs. He was nauseous and dizzy, and the singing was now an oppressive hum.

He was drunk on compressed air, the "rapture of the deep" that could be fatal if he didn't get to the controls. It was a narcosis that affected divers before him who had imagined themselves fish and torn off their masks to breathe the sea. Some did not survive to tell of their visions, as Colin knew he himself might not.

On the surface the air had pressed down on him with a weight of fifteen pounds per square inch. One fifth of that was oxygen, and air-breathers tolerated little deviation from that crucial three pounds.

He had tripled the air pressure in the cabin, and that tripled the oxygen pressure. Now he was hyperventilating, and the oxygen had become a poison for his brain.

He practically leaped for the controls and worked at them. The pressure gauges slowly dropped back to normal, and Colin took a deep breath in relief. The humming faded, his nausea eased, the room slowed its whirling and settled. The music in the room was once again the D major Horn Concerto.

It was good to be sane again.

Then Colin felt coldness at his feet. He looked down to find the water rising again, rushing in through the hatchway so fast he couldn't close it, creeping up round his legs, reaching for valuable circuits and switches. Horrified, he cranked the pressure up again pushing the water back out the hatchway.

Then once again the humming returned and the room started to whirl about him.

The dilemma offered him death with either choice. He had to get the oxygen pressure back to its normal three pounds per square inch and yet keep the overall pressure high.

His mind was growing soft, unable to focus.

... oxygen has to be 3 p.s.i. and total pressure has to be 45 p.s.i. ... oxygen at 3 p.s.i. and total pressure at 45 p.s.i. ... a dilemma ... not possible ... not with oxygen at 1/5 proportion ... then reduce the proportion ...

Reduce the proportion? Why not? One-third as much oxygen at three times the pressure would bring it back to the crucial 3 p.s.i.!

The oxygen fed from a separate valve and he dialed it down, reducing its proportion to one part in fifteen, an atmosphere so strange as to belong on another planet.

Slowly, very slowly, he drew a cautious breath, filling his lungs with air that would have suffocated him on the surface.

The strange air worked it way through his scarred lungs, through inflamed membranes into his blood, and finally reached his brain. The humming eased, the dizziness slowed. He cautiously breathed again, and the noise faded. Once again Mozart was only Mozart.

As his mind regained its focus the equation grew sharp. If he had gone up in a plane he would have had to increase the amount of oxygen in the cabin. Going down in the sea he had to decrease the amount. The deeper he would go, the less the amount.

Of course planes returned to earth sooner or later, but Colin would never return. He had chosen the depths for good, and even now each cell in his body and brain was being slowly and subtly changed. He was living in another world, filling himself with another world's atmosphere and learning another world's ways.

He would not know everything about that world, perhaps not ever, and certainly not immediately. However he had already succeeded in the most difficult task of all, he had broken through the barrier. He had turned back evolution and returned. Of course he expected to make a fair number of mistakes in his new—or ancient—home, but as he refilled his air tanks he was already anxious to step out that hatchway and know that freedom again.

Even his growing hunger brought him a sense of excitement. Of course there was some canned food but that was a limited store for emergencies. He expected he would live as his seal did, as another hunter of the deep. As the lynx prowled the forests, so he and the seal would be masters of their world.

He could hardly wait.

13 Fish were everywhere, endless varieties and crowded schools. Colin surveyed the field as he held his spear gun. A meal to be pan-fried lay at hand anywhere he pointed it, but he deigned to watch his seal first.

Bubbles of air streamed from her fur as she swam into a school of herring. They scattered, but not fast enough. She raced with them and suddenly lunged forward and swallowed one in a single gulp.

He closed in but the herring scattered as he approached. Frustrated, he turned on a larger jackfish but it seemed to anticipate his coming and glided neatly out of the way. He chased after a golden garibaldi but it was too small a target and he missed completely. He fired left and right, up and down at fish passing in every direction, but they seemed to know from where the spear was coming and he missed each one in turn. He chased after them, but they outdistanced him easily or ducked into small dark crevices.

Each time he fired he had to pull back the spear with the attached rope and take the time to reset the spear gun. By now the fish were wary, and soon they would not even come within range.

His seal still persisted in humiliating him by simply outswimming the fish and swallowing them easily.

A giant grouper lumbered by, a great striped fish with large sad eyes, and an even sadder thick-lipped downturned mouth. It moved its fifty pounds through the water easily though gracelessly, and curiously turned to Colin.

He took aim at the big target and fired broadside.

Suddenly the grouper was thrashing about, spear in its side and pulling spear, line, and an astonished Colin like a toy. On the surface, whales would tow whole boatloads of men for hours—a Nantucket sleighride. Here in a world of neutral buoyancy one small fish could do the same.

Colin held on to his prey with all his might, desperately grabbing at rocks for support while getting bumped and pummeled in the process. Still he clutched the line tight until the grouper retreated into a hole and turned, and with a clanking sound wrenched the spear into a neat right angle.

The fish disappeared into its grotto.

Bruised, bumped, exhausted, Colin swam slowly back to the sea-home.

Then he stopped. Just near the hatchway he saw two stiff feelers protruding out of a rock ledge. He swam down, pushed up the ledge, and found several lobsters gathered. They were night creatures and hid here from the daylight. Lacking the claws of their Atlantic cousins they looked quite helpless.

Colin, relieved, reached for the topmost one and picked it up easily, with the satisfaction of the hunter catching his living meal.

But Colin didn't notice the lobster's tail arcing down beneath his fingers, nor the line of sharp bony weapons buried within. The tail struck and the blades dug deep into his hand. Colin dropped the lobster and shook his wounded hand, weaving spirals of blood made strangely black by the water's green filter.

The slow current took the spirals, destroying their shape as a summer's breeze eventually shreds vapor trails in the sky.

A thousand yards downcurrent the designs diffused totally and spread wide in the tiny eddies and whirlpools formed among the various rocks.

Here and there was a stray particle, a remnant of remnants. There was no longer a visible trail. It had been washed away into the great ocean.

But now a huge shadow came by, a fearsome creation with a monstrous head swerving from side to side. Sensitive cells sifted great quantities of water seeking the tiniest change, any signal of helplessness or distress though its source be miles away.

Then that isolated tiny particle, a mere molecule of blood, passed through that system, and it was as if an alarm had been touched off through that huge body. All its nerves sprang to alertness and excitedly the creature turned into the particle's path.

Colin held his finger as he silently cursed both lobster and himself. He should return to the sea-home, unload his tanks and suit, bandage the wound, and then go through it all again just when food was at hand. Instead he put on his gloves, trusting them to close the wound for now, and reached again for the lobster, this time near the head beyond the reach of the vicious tail.

Colin certainly couldn't know that a mile away, a prehistoric monster, a nightmare to his own age, was speeding toward him.

Ages ago some daring fish worked its way ashore, seeking the insects or ferns just beyond reach, or perhaps driven on by mystic forces beyond understanding. As generations passed the creature evolved to a thick-skinned reptile, and after a hundred and fifty million years the reptile ruled the earth and sky. The lord among these lords was Tyrannosaurus Rex, the tyrant king of the lizards.

Men sometimes chillingly fancy the havoc such a creature could wreak in modern times, crushing automobiles with its ponderous legs, its great tail thrashing through brick walls, its claws grabbing screaming victims out of skyscraper windows, then devouring them cleanly with its dozens of razor teeth. Of course it is only a fantasy that vanishes in daylight, or when the lights come up in the cinema.

But the sea itself is the stuff of fancy and nightmares and the most powerful magic is wrought with its waters.

When the first reptile was developing, so was another oddity of the sea, and in that hundred fifty million years it too grew, and grew yet larger to the size of a giant while perfecting mechanisms and techniques of death. When the Tyrannosaurus Rex's kingdom was limited to the swamps, this other tyrant was a master in all the seas of the globe.

While the swamp tyrant had several limitations—it could hunt only by day, and could not help giving warning of its approach with its clumsy tail knocking over trees and rocks in a wide swath—the sea tyrant, quite as large and fearsome, just as powerful and destructive, hunted equally well in the dimness of shallow waters or the total night of the depths. It came swiftly and struck in silence.

On land, the earth shook in great convulsions as it cooled. The formerly warm humid weather went awry with cataclysmic storms, glaciers crept across the land, and the tyrannosaur's kingdom disappeared.

After a reign of fifty million years Tyrannosaurus Rex and his ponderous cousins died out leaving only miniature and modest relatives, lizards, snakes, crocodiles.

But in the depths of the sea there were no such storms nor ice ages. If there were earthquakes this creature was unaffected.

So while the monsters on land died, this one lived on, growing yet larger, honing its weapons, extending its kingdom, fortifying its rule, and waiting.

On land, rule passed to the mammals who in turn grew larger, until one grew so large it could no longer support its great bulk on land. And so the whale, the largest creature in all history, became the first mammal to return to the sea. But its size only made it a bigger feast for the tyrannosaur who attacked in a deadly movement too swift, silent, and sure to be called fury.

More tens of millions of years, and other mammals followed, the manatee, the dugong, seal, sea lion, sea otter, and each in turn met the same terror.

This creature developed a certain taste for mammal flesh, and it waited patiently through the ages of higher mammals and early apes, through higher apes and primitive man. It waited through countless cultures while civilizations formed, prospered, and died, and Man looked at the sea with strange longings, and made occasional trembling half-hearted forays.

Now, finally, after three hundred million years one man brought his destiny full circle and returned to his birthplace. And a monster glided swiftly and quietly along an invisible blood trail to meet him.

The lobster fought frantically as Colin pushed it into his bag.

He had just about worked it all the way in when he was suddenly bumped solidly from behind and dropped both lobster and bag. He turned around, vexed, prepared to scold a michievous seal.

He froze.

He was staring at the face and form of Death, for that was its true name, though the name men have given it is the shark.

They named this one the tiger, partly for its stripes, unusual among sharks, partly because men fear this shark particularly, as much as primitive man feared the tiger in the night jungle.

It is one of the most voracious of sharks, devouring sea creatures great and small, land animals stumbling into the sea, garbage thrown over a ship's side, and even inedible objects of plastic and metal. It seeks prey near the shallow waters of beaches, and at times even leaves its saltwater home to stalk miles upstream freshwater rivers.

At thirty feet it is a giant among sharks.

There are two larger ones, the basking and whale sharks, but they are gentle and placid, feeding only on microscopic life near the surface. They are anomalies, the scandals of this killer family.

The shark had followed the faint trail of Colin's blood for over a mile and ordinarily it would have attacked outright, but something was wrong and made the shark cautious. For one thing, this wounded mammal was not thrashing about in pain, as the shark knew before it saw its prey, knew it the same time it tasted the mammal's blood a mile off. Little hair cells in a fluid-filled canal along the shark's flank were sensitive to vibrations in the water. Perhaps all the vibrations of all the swimming creatures miles around were perceived as one smooth orchestration, while the disrhythmic thrashings of a wounded fish were as conspicuous, even at a great distance, as the single out-of-tune piccolo.

That thrashing alone would have brought the shark racing at thirty knots, for its taste was for the infirm, the weak, the wounded, the already dying. Even this formidable warlord plays no games of heroics, and "coward" has no meaning here.

But this new mammal was not thrashing about or bleeding at the moment, so with the instinct of three hundred million years the shark bumped Colin first, knocking him off balance, and at the same time tasting him with little crypts in its skin that were tied to its nose and tongue. Then it began circling, sweeping its head to and fro, and the movement flowed down the great body as on some slow thick eel.

But if Colin thought he could escape during that weaving and circling, the shark's eye held him frozen, its focus as sharp and firm as the lynx's eye in the zoo, amazingly stock-still in the midst of a fluid body. It reminded Colin that the maneuvering had one deadly purpose.

Thousands of years ago primitive man lit bonfires at night and never wandered outside the small circle the light carried. Beyond, in the darkness, lurked beasts of nightmarish ferocity, and though he was blind they were not and could find him in that darkness. Against their armored skins and fearsome weapons he had only the knife, the club, and the spear.

Man learned much in a million years. He conquered and tamed the land, developing complex technologies and tapping the power of the sun itself. But now he had returned to the sea, and in the diffusing dimness his most powerful electric lights penetrate little farther than bonfires on land. His most sophisticated weapons are either ludicrously sluggish or weak. Out there in that darkness lie prehistoric creatures, mostly unknown, with armories and senses denied him. They can find him and strike in this perpetual night, and against them his only weapons are once more the knife, the club, and the spear.

But now even Colin's spear gun lay empty beside him. This was probably immediately fortunate, for a spear would only have infuriated the creature and done no more damage than against a dinosaur, as Colin saw a moment later when the shark brushed up against the sea-home. There was a loud scraping noise and the metal was cleaned of its paint as if by some huge rasp file. The shark's hide, as tough and thick as sole leather, had in addition thousands of small pointed teeth, and had these come against Colin instead of the metal, his flesh would have been flayed to the bone.

He knew intuitively the futility of resistance and hoped only the end would be swift.

But as sharp as its senses were, the shark didn't hear Colin's surrender and continued to treat him warily, completing its first circle and starting a second one, closer.

The king had come with his court, several pilot fish that did not guide the shark, but rather accompanied him in hopes of sharing his meal.

Though thirty feet is surely a fearsome giant, where sharks a few feet long are deadly, it was not adult as humans think of the term, for sharks have neither adulthood nor childhood nor even helpless infancy. It hatched out of its egg inside its mother's uterus, and when totally born it was a fully developed shark in miniature, attacking prey of any size, lacking only its parents' caution and discretion. One species will even devour its brothers and sisters as they hatch in the womb so that only the most ferocious killer will be born.

It received no nurture at its birth. Its mother might have attempted to devour it herself depending on her temper or hunger.

"Come on," said Colin weakly to himself as the shark completed its second circle and started on a third, yet closer, weaving a web of invisible force, pulling it tighter about the trapped prey.

In part, that pattern of attack was born of the shark's anatomy, for from birth it had never rested, never ceased its motion, never slept. Lacking the air bladder of bony fish, the controllable air reservoir that allows them to stand still and hover, the shark had to swim or sink. More important, it lacked the breathing muscles that pumped water through the gills, and instead had to shunt water through them as it swam.

Yet what nature withheld was also its gift, for it gave this creature an invulnerability approaching the supernatural. Sharks have had bodies torn open, harpoons through the head, bullets near the brain, and have survived to attack again. They have been eviscerated, only to feed upon their own guts. They have lain on a ship's deck for hours, opened up, dried out, and dead by all human certainty, only to come alive thrashing, and snap a limb off a hapless sailor.

"Come on," said Colin to himself, but still the shark would not be hurried. It completed its third circle and started on its fourth, yet closer, pulling the web yet tighter, never for an instant removing its fixed gaze. Now it opened its mouth and showed its teeth in anticipation.

The tooth of the tiger shark is a razor-sharp dagger, roughly four inches long and serrated as the finest steak knife—a function it well serves when put in a handle. This single dagger in itself would be an awesome weapon, but in the shark it is multiplied by fifty, and these fifty are multiplied again by seven, for the shark has seven rows of fifty teeth. Should the one in front be lost, perhaps in its victim's body, the new tooth would work forward in a single day, larger than its predecessor.

In the attack the jaws would open wide and several dozen daggers would slice through rubber, metal, flesh, and bone at a pressure of almost twenty tons per square inch. Blood would gush out and its taste would excite the shark. The wild gyrations of a mortally wounded prey would whip that excitement higher. The shark would shake its head sideways, adding the weight of its body in a series of convulsions and transforming its teeth into power saws. In an instant a twenty-pound morsel would be sliced away cleanly, leaving a perfectly outlined semicircle in Colin's torso, now dancing crazily in death.

By now the shark would be in a total frenzy and almost instantly would take mouthfuls faster than it could swallow.

Even after the corpse was completely dismembered the frenzy would continue and the shark would snap at anything, other fish, other sharks brought to the scene, and even incredible objects in a lust gone insane, while the little pilot fish would nip hungrily at the tiny bits and morsels that fell from the shark's mouth.

Colin was enraged in his terror. It was cosmically unfair that he, a man, an intelligent creative human being, should have this priceless entity cut short so abruptly, cruelly, unjustly by a prehistoric parasite.

"Come on!"

A billion years of life, a million of humanity, ten thousand of civilization, all finished as so much meat on the hoof.

"COME ON!"

At last the shark turned out of its circle and headed toward him, its eyes still watching him steadily, its mouth opening to give Colin a view of that great cavern with shining white stalagmites and stalactites that would have him skewered between them.

The cavern opened wide, so wide it seemed to encompass eternity . . . and momentarily that darkness would close about him.

His rage grew till it suddenly found voice, pushed on and amplified by mortal terror. It exploded in a flash of white foam and bubbles, and at that same moment reached through Colin's muscles to his arms as they opened wide and slammed down on the striped roof.

It was as much a traumatic surprise to the shark as to Colin himself. The shark swung sidewise, and its great body tore against Colin as it swerved.

Even in surprise, the shark never stopped moving, wasted no motion but bent about swiftly and smoothly, speeding off into the dimness of the waters beyond, leaving turbulent swirls in its wake that sent Colin reeling backward.

Even its retreat was an expression of its power.

Colin knew the shark had taken measure of this new mammal. It would return, and not be surprised again.

14

It was exasperating.

Colin had the charts of the various currents on his desk and could make no sense of them. Various arrows bent about and crossed in meaningless patterns, and when he tried to set a course he would get lost in a tangle of lines, then he would hear the lobster scratching in its pot behind him. He would be reminded of the frustration in working it back into the bag with his hands trembling after his close call with the shark. Then he himself would tremble as he relived the whole incident, until finally he would look back at his charts to find he had added his own doodles to confuse them further, so he would be further back than when he started.

This had been going on for an hour or two when there was a splash at the hatchway, and his seal entered, pulling herself up by her flippers and crawling across the floor with a friendly growl.

Colin's delight at seeing her was cut short by the sight of a flapping sea bass in her mouth. He remembered its beauty and freedom, its scales catching the light in iridescent flashes, the first fish he saw so truly in its full life. Now it was writhing hysterically in her mouth, its color darkening even as Colin watched.

He thought of his episode with the shark, and for an instant *he* was that helplessly flailing fish, and her great bearlike teeth were clenched about *him*.

Suddenly those teeth sliced through scales, soft flesh and bone, and its spine snapped. In an instant its life was gone and it hung limply in her mouth.

Her long black shining nails dug beneath its skin and easily tore its scales off. Its head with eyes and mouth frozen in death was now in her mouth. She pulled with her flippers and tore the head from its body. This, the center of the fish's life and instinct, she dropped on the deck of the cabin. She swallowed the body in one gulp.

Colin's stomach turned, and he began to breathe hard. "OUT!"

She looked at him bewildered.

He pushed at her, shouting, until she retreated out the hatchway. He looked at the remains of the bass, the bloody head and scales, and kicked those out.

Revolted, he hobbled back to his charts, and tried to wipe the incident from his mind. He understood the shark as a remorseless mindless evil, but the seal ... her cruelty was the greater shock because she was not.

The lobster's scratching again distracted him, and Colin now saw a forlorn creature, as helpless as the seal when she was a pup, as vulnerable as the sea bass, as crippled as Colin himself.

And he would be eating it, breaking its spine, pulling out pieces of its meat, sucking out the insides ... Who now was the shark? Who now carried the evil?

Herein a paradox. He dropped back on his cot shaking, for he had discovered the true original sin, that man murders to eat, that he destroys life by living as surely as the specters that murdered the baby seals. Civilization had protected him with processes and packages, but now he saw it true. He had returned here to live as part of nature and at peace with it, but that only brought him closer to the killing.

To live at peace with nature was a myth, a delusion, a contradiction.

And yet, in some scheme of things he was meant to, for if he refused to kill he would starve to death and so do violence to himself.

He reached again for the volume of poems and found what he was looking for:

> *Fair mother, fed with the lives of men,*
> *Thou art subtle and cruel of heart, men say;*
> *Thou hast taken, and shalt not render again;*

Thou art full of thy dead, and cold as they.
But death is the worst that comes of thee;
Thou art fed with our dead, O Mother, O Sea,
But when hast thou fed on our hearts? or when
  Having given us love, hast thou taken away?

So she offered love in exchange for death. That was no bargain. He had known both, and love wasn't worth much. And death ... there was nothing more fearful than to die, nor more cruel than to cause another to die.

Thou art indeed cruel of heart, O Mother, O Sea, and why did he come here to find it?

He agonized for a long while until finally his eyes wandered to the hatchway. There was, of all things, a snowstorm outside, countless white flakes drifting past in silence. Isolated fish swam among the flakes, nipping at particles here and there like little children with their mouths open in a snowstorm.

What were they?

He leaned down the hatchway and scooped up a cupful in a beaker, put a few drops under his microscope and looked. What he saw riveted his eye to the lens in awe—almost disbelief.

A crystal casket floated by, filled with substances the size and color of jewels. It drifted slowly as if to a gentle waltz. Then came a crystal wheel revolving in that same silent tempo, its hub even more dazzling gems. Then came a series of spheres, each locked within another, designs within designs diminishing into infinity, puzzles Chinese artisans carved from ivory. There were others, more than he could count.

What were these wonders?

They were the smallest living things of the sea, single-celled plants that floated with the ocean's current, each in its own glasslike house.

Here was a multifaceted silver sphere like the ones that Colin remembered revolving on ballroom ceilings—a long time ago when he could dance. This one carried hundreds of tiny spines protruding from those facets. Then something troubling. One of the smaller crystal flowers was snagged by those spines and pulled into the sphere. The beauty was a destroyer of beauties.

A king's crown came to life as its coronas trapped another tiny crystal. Microscopic animals living off microscopic plants.

A dark shape clouded the microscope, and Colin pulled back to a lower-power lens. Among those tiny animals, this was a giant. Its body was a clear crystal with red and blue gems that were apparently its inner organs. Its antennae fluttered, securing particles of food, devouring coronas and silver spheres.

Now a minute cousin of the jellyfish, a blue light bulb pulling a tiny animal to its mouth by dangling red threads.

Then the larva of a crab, recognizably crablike though in crystal miniature, feeding upon another tiny animal. As the larva would grow, so its food would become larger.

Colin moved back farther, shifted to a yet lower power, and saw many such sea animals, all busily devouring their separate particles. Before him was a carnage, a holocaust. In that single drop of water lay a most troubling paradox.

He put the few drops back into the beaker where they joined the thousands of other motes, and the beaker back into the sea where they joined billions of others, became part of the great snowstorm called plankton, drifters of the world's seas.

As he poured it out, a silver arrow, a herring, shot by, feeding upon the plankton. Now more herring. Ten, twenty, a hundred in a swirl as complex as the chaos in his beaker, a sea of fish, their scales catching the light.

Then the hundreds of fish scattered, escaping bigger predators, squid.

Other fish joined the feed, cod, salmon, tuna, marlin, sailfish.

And then the great shark.

And even this king had his master. The long ceaseless swim of thirty years would eventually tire him. He would falter and his burdensome body would sink to the ocean's floor, no fresh oxygen for his gills, and he would suffocate and die on the soft ocean bed.

Eventually only his teeth would remain. The rest would join the steady rainfall of empty glass houses and the other dead creatures that had lived out their lives. All would eventually decay and become the graveyard of the sea.

So it ended with death. Death was all about him, in the smallest drop. He swam through slaughter.

Thou art full of thy dead, and cold as they.

He killed, and he himself would die. The final secret of life was death.

So this was the Siren's call after all. He should have taken warning from the Greeks who tied themselves to ships' masts or filled their ears with wax when they passed the Siren's isle.

And yet . . . wondrous murder, exquisite warfare, sublime death.

He stared at the death-filled waters until they darkened, becoming a rich blue, then violet, then black as the sunlight faded. Yet he knew the carnage continued even in that darkness.

The paradoxes spun around in his mind as the cabin darkened, until finally the darkness reached his mind and he fell into troubled sleep.

The darkness stretched out until it became a void without end, stretching to the far corners of the universe. Then far off there was a strange light, and with it that sweet singing.

He could not move. He could only watch as that light took form growing as it came toward him until it was monstrous, so huge that he could be crushed in its indifference.

It circled slowly, drawing its net tighter, coming closer and yet closer until it turned to him, its mouth opening to that great cruelty of countless daggers. The singing was very loud now, and he realized it came from within that cavern. He was being drawn to it even as it came for him.

He tried to yell, thrash about, strike back, but his body was a dead burden and hung limply, mesmerized by the song, welcoming death.

Those countless teeth closed about him and there was excruciating pain, unendurable and maddening as he felt a thousand knives pierce soft flesh, his bones cracking and crushing in upon each other.

As suddenly as it came upon him, the pain was gone.

He was at one with the creature that devoured him, atoms within atoms, mind within mind. He was now himself swimming through a kingdom of infinite green, a creature of grace and ruler of the sea as he danced to the song.

He danced till he tired, but the music would not stop nor let him stop. His body grew old and feeble, but still the music commanded. He cried for the sweet rest of death, tried to shut it out, willed himself to die, and finally sank to the gentle bed, the graveyard of the ocean's floor.

But the song followed, persisted, pierced his thick skin, broke through the closed brain and found him.

It came close, sang that he could leave that body and be finally totally free if he dared, if he would but give himself. He could survive death, exceed death, be reborn.

He listened, then he understood.

He was the song.

He was the sea.

He hit his head on the ceiling as he snapped awake. He tried to focus his eyes but the image they saw was bewildering, a cramped cot instead of his bed and a round green hole in the floor.

". . . oh . . ."

He shook his head to clear the grogginess. The dream haunted him and the song still throbbed in his head. At first he blamed it on the lobster he ate, but then he heard it scratching in the pot. He remembered he had not eaten it, had been afraid to. He still felt that fear, and deeply, but now there was a strange agitation with it as though another emotion was fighting in his brain to supplant it.

He looked down and saw his seal sleeping comfortably near him. He accepted her now in a way he had not before, just as he accepted himself in a way he had not. He could not understand why, though he sensed it grew from the dream.

He rubbed her affectionately on her soft neck. She

stirred, scratched her nose in an affectingly human way, and settled back to her slow even breathing.

Restless, he looked down through the waters of the hatchway. There was that same peaceful snowfall that was really a total war. Below, dozens of herring nipped at the motes, and below that, beyond Colin's vision, lay the great graveyard, the ultimate fact of the sea and of life.

Though fearful, he had to see. He strapped on his tanks and gear and dropped down softly, slowly into the sea.

He felt his body lighten again, exulted in the freedom given him. He exhaled, watched the bubbles rise and grow as the pressure lessened, changing colors as they caught the light. He relaxed and floated down through herring and squid that parted to let him pass and then swirled about him, until at last he reached the seabed.

Here the snowfall of a billion years had piled high the thick ooze on the bottom. Most of it was the silicate shells of the plankton, the teeth of sharks, and the earbones of whales since these were the hardest, and almost all else eventually dissolved. All life above from smallest cells to giant whales found their final rest here.

This was, then, the ultimate fact, the peace of death. There was nothing beyond that.

What had he hoped to find?

He let his legs give way beneath him, disburdening himself of thoughts and body. He fell softly into the ooze and it was stirred into a cloud that soon drifted off in the current. Idly, Colin mused how far it might be taken before being scattered and dissolving completely, and if it served a purpose.

He lay back and could not help wondering about his own dying at the bottom, his body dissolving and his cells joining the empty glass houses already here.

He was grateful he could not picture it. The image eluded him as if it were veiled by the sea, nature's way of protecting him. One should not be able to picture one's own death.

And yet . . .

He stretched his hands out and they touched something soft and spongy. Startled, he drew back and looked. It was indeed spongy for it was a sponge, an animal that seemed more a plant. It patiently waited unmoving all its life for the currents to push that snowfall through its pores. Nearby an oyster opened its mouth the merest millimeter to take in its food. Just beyond, a leathery sea cucumber crawled on needlelike legs like a centipede, while drawing the ooze into its mouth with encircling tentacles.

Colin arose, wandered through the graveyard, watched closely and saw other creatures that had made their homes here, either rooted in one place or crawling through the ooze to feed upon the feeders. A starfish had wrapped itself about an oyster and was calmly pulling with its suckered arms. Its force was not great, but it would pull for days until the oyster weakened and broke apart, and the starfish would push its stomach down into it for its meal.

Colin shoved aside a rock and found a lobster hiding from the daylight, picking apart a sponge.

He would eat the lobster as the lobster had eaten the sponge which had eaten the falling corpses of the rest of the chain, back to the plankton.

The chain was infinite. It circled and came back to where it began. Life flourished in the graveyard. Life was implicit in death just as death was implicit in life. A creature dies from the day it is born, but it lives from the day it dies.

Life and death were a duality, but also a unity. In eating the lobster, Colin would become part of that unity, that circle, living off it and having it live off him, taking nutrients, excreting nutrients. At the end he would join others in that graveyard, decay, his atoms dissolve, and he would be reshaped in other forms, other life.

The sea itself was a living thing, with this universe of living things within her, and he would become part of it, one more living thing.

Thou hast taken, and shalt not render again . . .

But she shall. He would be the plankton, and then all the creatures that lived off it. They would be the living cells within him, as he now had living cells within him. No matter whether he lived or died, he would still be part of her, at one with the sea.

He thought of his body decaying, the billions of cells

dying, his flesh growing moldier until he became merely molecules to be sifted through sea cucumbers and sponges. He shuddered.

Someday he might not. Someday he might face the fact of his death, give himself up to the sea totally and completely, pass into the ultimate darkness, that final barrier. Would he have some dim awareness of that new existence? Would he live that dream of himself as the sea?

Right now he would content himself with partaking of the great mystery in a small way. He returned to the cabin where the lobster still scratched helplessly against the pot. Did it understand on some dim but fundamental level as Colin understood? He turned on the electric coils underneath the pot and the water came to a quick boil in the high atmospheric pressure.

The lobster gave no hint it understood. It scratched frantically, tried to crawl out only to slide back in death.

But death is the worst that comes of thee . . .

Colin fell silent a long while. He had to get very hungry before he could bring himself to break open its spine and nibble its flesh.

. . . Just to be part of the sea. Subtle and cruel of heart. Would he ever get over that feeling?

15 The little animal scurried at dizzying speed across the night forest but the lynx was even swifter in its pursuit, bending its powerful legs and springing over brook and rock, landing so softly on padded paws it did not even hear itself touch the ground, rebounding so smoothly it fairly flew.

The prey was wily and elusive but no match for the sharpness of the lynx, its bright eyes penetrating the night, catching the slightest signs of the trail, its keen nose detecting the faintest remainders of the prey's passage. It was indomitable, omniscient, a creature of incredible grace, all its muscles quivering with the excitement of the hunt. The lynx was never more alive, never more its glorious self than at this moment, stretching its muscles, nerves, senses to their furthest powers.

The wily prey turned this way, that way, and saw its lair ahead beneath the protection of rocks and boulders. There was a clearing, and for one dangerous moment it would be totally exposed. With its final breath it jumped toward the rocks. The lynx was but a few feet behind . . .

"Damn!"

Colin was unable to turn in time and hit his head sharply against the rock. His head hurt badly and he was dizzy for several moments, but the humiliation hurt him even more. The lobster had simply outmaneuvered him. They were not only becoming scarce after several weeks, but the remaining ones were increasingly elusive.

Which brought up the question of Colin's fitness to survive. All he could catch was lobsters. If even they grew too wary and escaped . . .

Now Colin was getting quite hungry. He thought he could see it peering out at him from its hole. He moved his hand toward the hole and heard a scraping. The lobster was withdrawing to the farthest corner.

Colin had to be cautious now. If he reached in blindly and grabbed for the tail ... well, if lobsters were learning, so was he. First he put on the thick gloves and probed cautiously, making sure he would be touching antennae and not barbed tail. He maneuvered his fingers along the outer edges and felt only rock, then moved his hand slowly into the darkness.

It was important to capture it without too much movement or bleeding that would attract the shark.

He felt something that was not rock, that was definitely alive. Was it the antennae? Some sea cucumber or anemone? Should he grab it? It was so damnably difficult to tell with these gloves. Perhaps he should remove them. Perhaps he should simply wait until the lobster came out by itself, or try and hunt another lobster.

He would have done a number of things ordinarily, but he was hungry. He took a breath and probed deeper. He touched soft flesh. A living thing brushed around him, and suddenly his hand felt as if thrust into searing flame. Sharp thin teeth clamped down through the gloves, penetrated into the skin, and held on fast. He pulled out his hand, and with it came a four-foot moray eel, writhing angrily about him. He tried to grab it and shake it off with his hand, but still it hung on while thrashing, setting molecules of water dashing against other molecules, the energy racing across hundreds, thousands of feet of water far faster than sound waves, somewhere reaching interested sensors.

Even with his panic and pain, Colin managed to reach the spear gun, but the eel was twisting about him too violently for a good shot, nor could he get the gun back far enough to fire. Colin knew that far off the shark had already turned in their direction.

He used the spear gun as a handle and plunged the spear directly into the eel's body. Still it hung on. He jabbed it in again and again, and now the eel's blood was pouring out, sweetening the signals for the distant shark, goading it to come yet faster.

Now Colin could almost feel those waves himself.

Desperately he pulled and tore at the eel, and finally the jaw relaxed.

The eel danced a slow sinuous ballet as it drifted down in death spilling its blood behind it.

Suddenly Colin was slammed against the rocks by a powerful wind as a great shadow came. Before the eel had even reached the bottom the shadow opened its awesome mouth, breathed in, and the corpse was gone.

The shadow moved on and Colin shivered momentarily in relief. Another lesson learned. Morays were night creatures who spent their days in dark crevices. Not normally vicious, they resented intruders and Colin had stuck his fingers into the wrong hole.

He looked at his hand. The gloves were torn in long gashes that might have been his flesh, and he saw those sharp teeth could certainly have penetrated to the bone. And in an instant ... amputated and dying ... in an instant! He began to shake as the emotion finally caught up with the realization.

The sea was no paradise. There was no food for him, no place for him in its scheme. He was an outsider and every step was a trap, every dark place an ambush. Nor was death the pleasant rest of the graveyard, but a pain far beyond the searing heat and mangling shock of the explosion. Instead, his flesh would be neatly skewered, his limbs scissored, and if he lived long enough he would watch his blood and insides pouring out. It would happen any place, anytime, without warning and in an instant.

Meanwhile his hunger was growing greater. Death by either means, slow or quick, seemed certain.

Now his shaking was a convulsion. He turned about to watch the diminishing shadow, and at that same moment, as if by telepathy, the shark turned and faced him again. Its baleful green eye focused on him and Colin retreated in horror.

Frantically he looked for a crevice, any place in the rocks to hide. He clawed desperately among the reefs, all reason, all caution vanishing.

It was as if an electric shock passed through the shark, and it sped directly toward its human prey.

Colin pulled himself between boulders just as the shark reached him. Furiously it flung itself against the rocks, and the bed trembled as if in an earthquake. Colin cowered against the farthest corner of that crevice, and he could see through a slit in the rocks the awesome shadow wheeling about for another attack. This time the shark rolled on its side as it passed, opening its mouth as if to bite the rocks and Colin in one huge mouthful, and at the same time giving him another view of those awesome daggers. He saw that glowering eye study him as it passed, and it set him into a new rage. Why him?

The shark circled about for yet another pass, its weaving head leading the streamlined body.

Colin's fright faded in his fascination, and he realized it was that malevolent eye that had terrified him, and made him swim for the rocks.

Astonishingly, calm now settled on the shark just as Colin's panic settled, for after some desultory brushes against the rock it turned and swam lazily away.

Colin cautiously pushed his way out of the crevice to watch how the other creatures reacted as the shark came near. The fishes in its path neither panicked nor scurried as the shark passed. Instead they respectfully cleared a path for the king. It took small notice of them, and they of the shark. The shark swam on.

About Colin the sea and all its creatures were calm. He alone trembled and had been conspicuous in his panic, once again the out-of-tune piccolo in the smooth orchestration. It was his panic that had attracted the shark, disturbing the nerves in its fluid-filled canals, conveying falsely that Colin was ill or infirm and ready to die. As long as his behavior was calm and well, the shark would take no notice.

He saw now that all fish behaved this way. He noticed that when the tuna moved slowly and calmly among the herring, the smaller fish sensed their predator was not hungry and made no attempt to escape.

So this was the way to hunt.

He had learned how to return to the sea by following the ways of the seal. He would learn how to survive from all the creatures. Empirical knowledge, yes, but much more. He was learning as the ancients dreamt of learning, by reading the sea's language and listening to its voice, and if he opened himself totally he might be given total wisdom.

With his spear at the ready, he moved out slowly and quietly toward the tuna, making no quick or abrupt movements, waiting rather for the tuna to get close to him, and when close enough he let his spear fly.

He hit it dead center. He had succeeded. He had returned and become part of the sea.

His exhilaration faded as he watched the tuna die slowly and agonizingly, spilling its blood in spurts of intense thrashings, its mouth gaping in a soundless scream.

It died slowly, and its fins shuddered with the convulsions of its body and gills. Gradually it weakened. The gasps were shorter, and its twistings about the spear diminished to quiverings. Its gills caught on one breath, froze, and there was a sudden single shake of its entire body. Then it relaxed slowly as death crept across its length.

And yet it was as necessary that the tuna die as that Colin live. If he must kill he would do so quickly, without delight, as a necessity and not a sport.

He would be humane in his killing as the beasts were, rather than bestial as the humans were. To kill no more than necessary he had to make use of every part of the creature he had taken. He would have to kill quickly and painlessly, in vital spots between the eyes or behind the gills.

So in the days that followed he had to practice endlessly to become a better shot, and he learned from the creatures about him.

From the frogfish, a creature that dangled a fleshy-looking appendage to lure a fish closer, he learned to wave his glove at a fish to do the same.

To respect regeneration he varied his diet widely, so he ate whatever he saw his seal eat—herring, salmon, greenlings, turbots, squid, sand lance.

If he approached a nesting female, small and apparently harmless, she swam at him viciously, waving her flimsy fins frantically, trying to bite him with comically small teeth. He was moved and awed by her pitiful desperation and respected it. It seemed the sea was letting him know what he must not take.

If in fact he thought of himself as a lord of the water, deciding who should live and who should serve to let him live, he had to be reminded of his true place. If he stepped incautiously on some clay ooze, the ooze itself might come to life and strike him painfully with a miniature mace, and the skate, a small manta ray, would fly off.

If he picked up a beautiful Conus shell to admire its intricate and vividly colored spirals, he would risk being speared by a poisonous dagger suddenly thrust from the shell.

Even the tiny plankton had their warriors, the sea mosquitoes that fed on Colin's flesh should he wander carelessly among them.

And over them all was the great shark, coming where and when it chose, wandering through its kingdom at will, with none disputing its right.

If Colin grew lax, if he did not kill swiftly and surely so that his fish neither thrashed about nor spilled too much blood, the shark was usually there to confiscate the prey, and Colin would have to let it lest it take Colin as well.

Gradually he came to behave as the other creatures. He learned when wandering in strange territory to hug the rocks closely; to cast frequent looks behind him (and since an assailant could move in three dimensions, Colin would also have to look overhead and underfoot); to reach cautiously for a handhold or step lightly on a foothold lest "it" come alive; to jump for safety at any unexpected motion or sound, much like any fish. And he never put his hands in dark holes.

But against the shark there was no sure answer, no precaution. Its only rule was its absence of rules. Perhaps in some great scheme the ultimate predator could not be bound by rules to be discerned by lesser creatures.

The shark would come upon him silently and unexpectedly, for there are no sounds of footsteps in the sea. Colin would be hiding behind a rock, waiting for a fish to approach, and would be suddenly startled to find the shark waiting behind *him*. It would finally swim off in its own time, neither threatening to attack, nor cowed by yells, bubbles, or slaps as it had once been. It was coming to know this new sea mammal and it would come for Colin when it was ready. For now, it seemed to come only to remind him.

Colin hated the shark as one can only hate the reminder of death, especially now when he was beginning to feel so very much alive. He came to the graveyard again, to see the master even of sharks.

As he wandered through the soft ooze and kicked up the clouds, again he noticed how the current took up the cloud and sent it south.

To what? To where?

His charts told him he was traveling the great clockwise-turning circle of the Pacific and that wondrous new kingdoms awaited.

He tired of this graveyard. He called to the seal, took her aboard, turned the metal sails of his craft to catch the currents, and drifted with them as the white clouds drifted.

They drifted southward in that part of the current called the California Current and came to a strange and splendid place, fed by the white clouds, by the graveyard of the place he had come.

Here was an awesome golden green forest, stretching from the rocky bottom to the surface sunlight a full hundred feet above. When dead this kelp washed ashore as so much damp blackish straw that entangled Conlin's legs, but here it was great golden trees undulating sinuously, held aloft by little air-filled pods. Colin imagined himself a bird suspended above a forest while other birds in the rolling branches peeked out at him.

The most common of these was the garibaldi, a short-tempered little gold fish, staking out its own territory, and nipping at and driving off any foreign creature, including Colin.

Many of the animals hid near the bottom, where the kelp was anchored to the rocks by suction cups, but Colin needed only shake a frond near its support and a multitude of life would fall out together, cuttlefish, barnacles, crabs, mussels, shrimp.

The sea urchin clung to rocks while feeding off the kelp,

defending itself with a formidable array of sharp, long spines.

A clump of seaweed moved independently along the bottom. But this was the decorator crab that carefully selected assorted plants, plucked them with its claw, and transplanted them to its back for camouflage.

When not watching the many wonders of life within the forest, Colin would stand enraptured at the spectacle of the forest itself, the awesome hundred-foot trees slowly writhing in the currents, illuminated by flickering shafts of sunlight.

His only fear and hatred remained for the shadow that came at its own times.

"Not yet, not yet!" he would say to himself, but the shark would circle about, drawing closer, inspecting him with its fixed eye, then turn off to swim away.

The seal gave little mind to the shadow and none at all to her own distant end. She lived her life entirely in this moment and place, her senses charged with the excitement of the hunt, or exulting in the tickling of water swirling about her as she swam, or simply creating endless games for herself, like keeping aloft some shell with her nose, diving beneath it just before it would settle to send it aloft again.

Colin would watch her for a long while and wish he were a child again, but then he would remember that childhood ends, that life ends, and he would think again of the shadow.

At last Colin turned the metal sails of his sea-home, caught the current again and sailed away from death. He sailed to where the various currents met at the Equator and headed west together in the flow called the Central Equatorial Current, the basic flow of all the seas.

From the soft and muted colors of the kelp forest he came to a place of almost blindingly vivid hues, of reds, purples, blues, yellows, and others he could not even name, spread out in a Turkish rug of countless miles.

But this life too was built on death. The tiny coral polyp, an animal much like the anemone, extended its wriggling tentacles out to the currents, caught and killed the passing plankton, and from this built a lime house about itself. Then the corals joined together by the dozens, hundreds, thousands in strange and glorious configurations.

Here they were twisted into branches, with the branches twisted into more branches until they resembled complex horns of stags, and so they were called staghorn corals.

There, joining themselves differently, secreting different colors, they resembled a stone sculpture of a human brain, with ridges of brown and fissures of violet, and so they were called brain corals.

Sometimes they joined to form seeming plants, daisies wrought by some artisan working in precious metals who created stalks of gold and petals of silver.

Against these brilliant colors swam sea creatures of more brilliant colors, as if a mischievous child had taken a coloring set and painted them all. Here were leopard-spotted snails ... a sea bass in red and gold ... the lion-fish striped in red and white like a barber pole ... a giant clam with flesh of iridescent green, blue, purple, brown . . . the crown-of-thorns starfish with its nineteen arms of orange and yellow.

The coral reef was a great city, a thousand-mile sponge to house the myriad creatures that lived within it, or off it, or off each other.

Colin came to regard these as his friends, even the moray eel. He could hold out a morsel of food, and gradually it learned to feed from his hand. Then others of endless and varied rainbows clustered about him. Some laid their eggs in the crevices of his home, or swam near the hatch where they knew he would appear.

They were all of the brotherhood of creatures, and if he had to kill them so he might live, to himself he would ask their forgiveness, and remind them they would live again in him as someday he would live again in them. He said it so often it eventually became a ritual, and the ritual became a chant, and the chant a song.

But the shark was not a part of this communion. It remained unaffected, to travel alone, the shadow that came for the weak, the infirm, the dying, and someday for Colin.

And someday for the seal, though she gave no sign she knew, no more than any child.

To keep his mind from that knowledge, Colin filled it

with new substance. He sailed to far places, taking the counterclockwise currents south of the Equator, coming at last to the Antarctic where the ice glowed above him a soft blue-white, washed with the yellow and brown pastels of plankton. Below, white crystals glistened austerely on the black volcanic rock.

Even in these cold waters life was thick and rich, fed by the distant currents, by death. It was a similar play with a different cast. Instead of herring there were tiny red lobsters called krill, small enough to fill the sea by the trillion, but large enough to be seen and eaten by whales and penguins.

He looked on the penguins as his cousins, waddling comically on land, flapping stubby wings helpless to lift fat bodies. Yet in the water they too were creatures of grace. Their portly bodies buoyed them up easily, their stunted wings were really flippers that took them speedily beneath the ice to grab the tiny red krill with ease.

There were other seals, nosier than his own. Weddell seals, leopard seals, crabeater seals, and their chirps filled the sea.

And over this richness of life again swam the shark, impervious to the cold, winnowing out the weak whether the greatest of whales or the smallest of fish—or the most malformed of men.

There was no escape, not in this world.

Then one day Colin came to the place where the world ended.

16 He stood trembling on the ocean's floor at the edge of the world.

Behind him the bright shafts of sunlight played upon vividly colored fish and living reefs. Ahead lay the great chasm where the planet dropped away into eternity, where lay an unknown world.

Here there be lions, warned the ancient map-makers of the unknown places, black seas, thick jungles that lay beyond the edge. What creatures of nightmare lay down there more terrible than forgotten lions?

Down in that darkness the cataclysmic forces that created the planet were still at work, heaving aside great mantles of rock in undersea quakes, setting endless volcanoes erupting in the "Ring of Fire," forming new crust in geologic birth throes. If the planet were a living creature, miles down in that blackness surely lay its womb, seven miles deep, a place of unimaginable pressures, cold, and eternal blackest night.

He quivered, trying to see into that darkness, straining to read the sea's image and hear its voice. Did that black silence speak of death, or escape from death?

And then he heard it, from out of that deep, a singing, strange and modal, of almost unbearable beauty.

I will go down to her, I and none other . . .

Below, in that darkness, lay no pain, no crutches, no torment, sweet rest.

Close with her, kiss her, and mix her with me . . .

Suddenly he awakened. He thought he had gone mad, plunging over the edge of some great cliff at the bottom of the sea and hanging suspended magically over some awesome chasm.

The blackness came up to envelop him and then he was immersed in it, pulled down into eternal depths. He tried to scream but the blackness came in through his mouth and reached deep down for his lungs.

With one last bit of strength in some far corner of his soul he screamed, clawed frantically at empty water, tried to wake up in his bed on land with his legs crippled and his body a torment, but there was no awakening and this was no dream.

He saw a shaft of light ahead and reached for it. He grasped it gratefully, then another, then a mass of gold-green light, and soon the reassuring seabed was beneath his feet. He floated down on his back and lay there a long while, slowly warming in the sun.

He had felt the cold sliminess of the great darkness. He had touched death.

From a safe distance, he stared at the awesome canyon. Could there possibly be a light somewhere beyond?

> *Thou hast taken and shalt not render again;*
> *Thou art full of thy dead, and cold as they.*

He shuddered. "Not yet. Not yet."

17 It is believed among peoples who have known the seal that a human spirit lives beneath the skin, that she may cast off that skin and come ashore among men, marry the one she loves and bear him children. But then she may well be torn between her homes and children of the sea and of land. At times her voice may be heard at night, weeping for her fate. She may finally put on her skin again and return to the sea, and her lover will be left mourning on the shore, or will drown in following her.

But in this time and place one man did follow. He put on his sealskin of foam rubber and glass and metal, and went with her to her kingdom.

At times they would just hover quiet and weightless together, while staring up at the shifting colors of the surface above, and he would soon forget there was a world on the other side.

She had a varied vocabulary of sounds, and he was learning subtle differences even within them.

Then he would hear the many other sounds of the sea ... the chatterings of little shrimp snapping their claws together ... the whistles and squeaks of herring gathering in schools ... the croaker fish drumming on its air bladder ... the distant plaintive songs of the great whales. Sometimes the whole sea sang with harmonies that would be inconceivable to Mozart.

He was still more a part of land than of water, and though he dreamt of throwing off these new crutches, of being totally naked and free in the depths, he would still have to return to his sea-home, refill air tanks, and be weighed down for a time with earthly weight and pain again. The seal still gave him reason for envy.

The barrier, that solid interface between air and water, seemed to fade and it all seemed one medium, one element. More and more frequently he would forget to put on his tanks and diving suit before venturing out, and a paroxysm of coughing and sputtering would remind him water was still not his natural element.

Yet, the sea was changing him. It forced his thoughts down to the narrowness of this place and this moment. Only near objects were visible in the waters. Beyond that was the past, the places he had been, or the future, where he was going. These were a blur, and they eventually became the irrelevant unperceived background.

By contrast, that which was at hand became more important, immediate, tangible, until he perceived time and space as she did.

Soon, like her, he discovered new joys in his senses. There were endless subtleties in tastes and textures of his food and the act of eating itself, all upon buds that had once been overwhelmed by heated gases and had never dared taste again. In turn, the other senses were awakened, magnified and attuned in strange new ways until they might someday reach together the most complex and simple sense of all, of being.

He had a clock aboard that had reminded him of earthly urgencies, working hours, production quotas, things to be done and things left undone, ticking away a desperate and wasted life. Now that clock ran down and he never noticed for he lived more intensely in nature's time, as did all creatures with inner clocks that regulated countless body functions still mysteries.

All life that is touched by time responds to its rhythms. The smallest, simplest plants and animals possess these inner mechanisms that tell them when to mate, spawn, sleep, feed. Even when removed from the outdoors and the guidance of the sun, and placed in light-shielded laboratories, certain worms remember their cycles, responding to unseen days and nights.

Colin still saw day and night, but here it was thrillingly different. An unseen sun moved across an invisible sky, and the ceiling of Colin's world would slowly pass from bright gold-green to deepest black. The reds of sunset and sunrise were absorbed by the water, but he was given instead new subtleties, colors within colors.

Day creatures withdrew into their nests or burrows and night creatures came out, those less well protected whose thickest cover was the night. The octopus slithered along rocks in search of its prey. The snowfall of plankton turned upside down and fell up, rising to catch the surface currents that carried them back to their starting point.

After a while, Colin began to feel the changes in tempo of these daily rhythms as the seasons changed. There would be a feeling of excitement, of quickening as warming waters of spring began rising, pulling up nutrients from the bottom, and soon the sea would turn red or brown or green with new microscopic life.

During summer the waters ran riot with the vast migrations from nurseries to spawning grounds.

The tempos slowed with the autumn when all dwindled and creatures deserted or died, and a torpor grew over the sea.

In winter the waters turned gray and lifeless. He could feel them heavy with coldness and death, sinking in mournful procession to the graveyard at the bottom, and the tempos so slow and funereal as to practically cease altogether. But then at the bleakest moment the waters began their rise, bringing life out of death, and the circle was brought round.

There was however another set of rhythms, at times converging with the first, at times diverging, but far more subtle and vast, for the sea responded to the pull of bodies outside itself.

There were the twice-daily surges of the tides that initially matched the days, but gradually grew out of synchronism, advancing a little bit each day as the moon orbited the earth. There were monthly variations as the moon came in line with the sun and they pulled the sea together, or when on opposite sides of the earth they pulled the sea between them.

There were yet subtler variations in the more distant pulls of the planets and their satellites in their slow turnings about the sun. Finally, since each particle in the universe responds and influences all others, there was the slowest, most subtle and cosmic dance of all, the smallest drop of water and its atoms responding to all the matter and energy of the universe.

There was a tie between inner space and outer space, the smallest parts of the smallest cells within Colin and the great galaxies, the infinitesimal and the infinite, the final circle brought round. He did not perceive it yet, but it gradually began to seem that his life and his death were rather trivial, and very, very important.

When he stared at the endlessly shifting sparkles of the ceiling of the water world he felt serene behind the glass barrier, protected forever from the world above. He was at peace.

Then one day they found his world.

18 They broke through the ceiling and shattered it. First came the propellers that sliced the ceiling into countless fragments and allowed the great nets to trawl through the sea, sweeping up tuna, herring, salmon, greenlings, turbots, squid, and sand lance. The dredges scraped the bottom and took oysters, lobsters, clams, sea cucumbers, skates. They took males and females, full grown and larvae, homes and nests, all they needed and all they did not need. The latter were thrown back, wounded, crushed, spines broken, mouths in silent screams, gills torn, skins ripped. Then the nets and dredges moved on.

The whaling ships came next, driving the terrorized herds to the surface, harpooning them with two-hundred-pound shafts that were fired from cannons, kept lodged in the flesh by barbs, and fitted with grenades that exploded organs or blew out huge chunks of blubber and blood. The whales had voices to scream and they screamed for hours until they died.

Then came the men-fish themselves, with scubas, masks, rubber suits, and spear guns. They competed to spear the most fish in the shortest time, spearing golden garibaldi, sea bass, lion-fish, firing at anything that moved or showed color until the water ran red.

They moved on, replacing those kingdoms with their own—bottles and cans, wooden boxes and rubber tires, odd parts of machinery, corroded pistols and cannon shells.

They also left papers of plans for the future, telling how much more efficiently they would do what they had done, and begin things not yet begun. They would open resorts under great glass domes, dredge up the seabed and the fish with giant vacuum cleaners, drill beneath it for undiscovered ores, and fight more efficiently with missile deployments, submarines, and fortresses in hollowed-out mountains.

So now they had found Colin's world, and there was no place for him to go, not in any of the currents nor in any of the seas.

Except one.

Again he felt crippled as he stood above a new world looking at the barrier beneath, only now the glass was black instead of silver.

Once before he had tried to pass through it and failed, but he had since grown closer to the sea.

Again he listened, and he heard the song.

> *O fair white mother, in days long past ....*

He would leave them and go where they would never follow, seven miles down in that great unknown of dark cold and pressure, of seething volcanoes and earthquakes where the planet is still being born.

> *Born without sister, born without brother ....*

He maneuvered the sea-home over the chasm, and folded the sails flat against the bulkheads, for he no longer would control the craft by the currents. His path was straight down. He opened the valves that first sank the sea-home, only now he opened them all the way. Again ballast tanks squealed and moaned as they gave up the remaining air. The huge air bubbles rose speedily as if fleeing from a madness, the sea-home began its downward voyage into the great darkness.

> *Set free my soul as thy soul is free.*

He grabbed for a handhold on the side, and his seal swam down after him.

A school of ever-present herring scattered as the craft drifted down among them, and then through them. A giant grouper stared at the sight of what seemed to be a strange cubed sea creature, spilling bubbles as it descended while two mammals hovered about it like pilot fish.

The water changed from green to a darker blue-green as the life-giving colors of the sunlight were gradually subtracted. Ominously, the plants and coral that grew along the rocks began to diminish in number, the fish grew sparser, the rocks craggier and more tortured.

Colin looked above him. The gold-green waters, the warm shafts of sunlight, the rippling ceiling were all receding into the distance. The retreating bubbles caught the light as they neared the surface like little silver suns, growing larger as they rose, distended into pear shapes by the pressure.

The blue grew darker and purer. A cataract of flowing sand ran down around cragged rocks, a strange reversal of earth flowing through water.

He looked below and saw a disquieting sight just where the blueness was its most intense. The waters were in ferment, shimmering like heat waves in air, and he was descending straight toward it.

The seal drew back. There was something fearful about that turbulence as if it formed the ceiling of another world, as indeed it did. Upper waters were stirred together as they rose and fell with their changing temperatures, but here in the deeper seas the difference in temperature was so great that they no longer mixed. The lighter warm water Colin had lived in sat upon this deeper cold water as a separate layer, and the line between them was as stormy as any border between weather fronts.

The sea-home hit the surface wave of the separate ocean beneath, and bounced like a rubber ball upon this thermocline.

Then Colin himself hit the layer, bounced, and then he hung there suspended as, a long time ago, he had hung suspended on the ocean's surface, unable to sink. He would have to wait until his rubber suit cooled to the temperature of the water below. The steel craft cooled faster and started sinking in levels, like a hot iron through ice.

Colin turned up to his seal and signaled her to follow, but she pulled away even as he began sinking through the layer himself.

"Don't be afraid. Come on!"

She swam toward it and backed off. To her it was an impenetrable barrier, as indeed it was to most sea life. The turbulence itself frightened her, but it also warned of the waters beneath. Most of the oxygen was in the upper ocean, stirred into it by the surface winds and given off by the plankton, but both stopped short at this border. A surface fish that braved the border and ventured below would actually drown. A seal whose lungs were not fed by pressurized tanks would soon be crushed. Below that line lay another ocean, another creation as strange as a different planet.

Already Colin could feel himself growing heavier. He looked down at his sea-home sinking out of sight, and up at his seal still trying to follow him and backing away in fright.

"Come on!"

He looked at his dials; his own air was rapidly vanishing. He had to get into the home.

He passed the barrier completely, and now he was falling freely away from her. Helpless, he watched her recede in the distance, a frenzied silhouette against a green sky. She grew smaller and smaller, seeming now the frail pup he first found, frightened at her first time in water.

Then she was lost to sight.

Stunned, he finally flipped his legs as she had taught him, and dove down after the craft.

He caught a handhold, and worked his way down and around, coming up through his open hatchway beneath.

Water was flooding in from the greater pressures and rising in the sea-home. He pulled himself to the console and frantically adjusted dials, increasing the pressure to match the outside, then cutting down the proportion of oxygen to keep it at that critical three pounds per square inch, down to fractions so tiny they could barely be read on his dial.

By the light of his sea-home he watched the ever more bristling rocks and crags, twisted and pushed into incredibly sharp shapes by the cataclysmic forces of a still settling planet, and never smoothed by surface winds and rains.

The lamps of the sea-home were an isolated warm spot in the cold violet-blue darkness, and they brought light to the great slabs of rock nearby that had not seen light since the earth was born.

The craft was a firefly drifting down a canyon deeper, grander, more raw than the Grand Canyon or any canyon on land. It was surrounded by other peaks and promontories, great grooves and trenches. Nearby, a sand river broke free over a precipice to become a majestic sandfall of several hundreds of feet, losing the lighter sand in a dissipating cloud. Some of the peaks rose to the green of the surface waters, or broke through to become islands. In the distance there was what seemed to be a sunset, and far beyond were several more. These were miles-high volcanoes, belching fire and lava and gases in giant glowing bubbles that rose to the surface.

It was like a vision of Hades, and indeed one name of the abyss is the "hadal" zone. Colin had rejoined his primitive beginnings when he returned to the sea, and now he was going back further, to the birth of the planet itself.

The single overwhelming aspect of the sea was its total and pure blackness. Even the sunlight penetrating a half-mile into the sea, its color ranging from green to deep violet, made small headway into seven miles of that pure night. Yet in a strange way there was a familiarity about it. Colin might have been looking at a mirror image of an evening sky, the reddish glow of sunset near his horizon, the progressive colors of the spectrum stretching out beneath, and beyond that the night.

Now the final bits of violet disappeared from his viewing port, and he crossed the border into that pit.

He noticed the clock that he had let run down, and now wished he hadn't. The last thread to the world as he knew it had been severed for that clock could never be reset, and time as he had once known it no longer existed. The abyss was beyond the reach of any of the cycles by which time is perceived. There was no day or night, no progressions of the sun or moon or stars, no changes of tide, no seasonal changes of warm and cold. There was only endless timeless cold and darkness.

The traveler who flies across time zones is "not himself" for days until the many mysterious body clocks readjust themselves to new times of day and night. Here not only time had faded, but space as well. In that endless emptiness there were no landmarks, no dimensions, nothing to distinguish here from there.

The only two forces that could be felt were coldness and the awesome weight of all the water above. On land, Colin had lived under a mountain of air perhaps a hundred miles high that pushed down on him with a total weight that was equaled by a mere thirty-three feet of water. At the bottom it would be over seven tons per square inch, the weight of seven miles of water.

For a creature born here there could be no light, therefore no plants, therefore almost no oxygen. Neither were there nests or territories. There would be only numbing cold, crushing pressure, and unending total night. It was small wonder life here was thought impossible.

And so Colin came to believe, for light, space, and time no longer existed.

And the earth was without form, and void; and darkness was upon the face of the deep. And the Spirit of God moved upon the face of the waters.

These were those waters, the sea of chaos that existed before Creation, before the universe.

Then Creation began, but differently, warped and distorted. A strange creature came into view resembling the sea cucumber of the ocean graveyard, but this one swam flapping a fringe along its side. It brushed against the glass and suddenly ejected its insides through both ends in a mass of mucus threads that swelled into a net to entangle its prey.

As Colin compressed the air in his home to keep pace with the outside pressure, it grew hotter. He tried to fan himself with a sheaf of papers, but the air resistance was so great the papers tore to pieces.

He looked at the depth gauge. One mile.

A long thin eel drifted by, as transparent as if it were made out of some kind of plastic film. Its organs were visible, and Colin could see its food digesting.

He tried fanning himself with a sheet of metal. Nothing happened at first, but then a second later a violent gust of wind practically threw his head back. The molecules of air were bunched closer together, and it took several seconds for the disturbance to work its way across the room where it knocked over books and instruments. He let them rest, and returned to the window.

Silence and darkness.

Suddenly the home was rocked and shaken as if by some huge hand. Contents of the shelves fell and slid across the cabin deck as the craft plunged downward as if the water had suddenly vanished underneath. With an earsplitting sound, cracks suddenly opened and spread through the craft, and water began seeping in. A terrified Colin worked his way across to the console and increased the inside pressure. Gradually the craft settled and the seepage stopped.

He had hit the deep-sea equivalent of the downdraft that can send a huge airliner hurtling down hundreds of feet in seconds. In the sea there are great undersea waves hundreds of feet high, a surging of dense water against light water, and the undersea craft caught in that wave suddenly finds itself grown heavy and slides down that mountainside. More than one submarine thus fell beyond its depth and was crushed.

There was darkness again for a measureless while, and then a nightmare swam past the window and turned, attracted by the light. The mouth was enormous, occupying much of the head, and when that mouth opened it revealed rows of teeth that were long, curved and sharp. Dangling above and below its head were strange long growths.

Colin stared, hypnotized, waiting for it to come closer, dreading the thought he might have to face such a monster. But then the creature bumped up against the glass, and Colin breathed in relief when he saw it was but a few inches long.

Two miles.

Then lights. For a moment Colin thought he was falling through the heavens, for ahead he saw the stars, endless constellations that weaved and shifted even as he watched, and in colors of red, blue, yellow, green, set against the pure blackness.

Strange ghostly forms hovered in the distance. A brilliant animated comet flashed by. A tiny green light slowly grew until it filled his view, then diminished and vanished. A red light brushed against the porthole and exploded in a bright shower of sparks.

Darkness again.

Three miles. Four. Endless darkness for timeless time.

Suddenly a flapping noise. It grew more intense until it was a pounding as if someone or something was trying to get in. A frantic Colin pushed his hands against the porthole as if that would hold back the tons of water.

Then a huge undulating form, a mass glowing a dull green. The next moment the entire ship was lifted and tilted, and Colin went sprawling. He tried to reach the controls but the ship tossed violently. There were creaking sounds in every joint in the hull, and Colin looked about frantically at each trouble spot.

Suddenly there was a rifle shot, or what seemed like one. A bolt gave way and flew across the room with the sound and impact of a bullet. It narrowly missed Colin and ricocheted off the opposite wall with a clang, followed by a needle spray of water, as sharp and straight as a laser beam, that bounced back and forth across walls with a high-pitched scream.

Then a second bolt gave way and shot across the room, flattening the controls as if they were clay. Then a third bolt, and the steel housing of the machinery caved in like a paper house. The lights began fading and the hissing of the air regenerator slowly died.

The sea-home was useless now, a tomb if he stayed here longer. The portable tanks gave him his only tiny threads to life.

To reach them he had to hug the floor, edging carefully around the needle sprays that would have sliced through him cleanly. As he crawled he pushed compressed tons of air, and the molecules gave way reluctantly.

The water on the floor did not splash but rose sluggishly like thick oil, forced back down by the almost equally heavy air.

Gasping, every move an effort of slow-motion agony, he finally managed to get on his gear.

He reached for the spear gun, and just as the final light

died he remembered the book with the poem. On an impulse, he tore out the page and stuffed it in his suit.

Then he dropped out of the hatchway into the blackness below.

19 The weight of miles of water crushed the home of metal and glass like a matchstick toy between giant hands, a vise of unimaginable force.

But it did not crush Colin.

If a block of wood is lowered a mere mile into the depths, it comes back crushed to half its thickness, with the harder knots protruding like stumps in a leveled forest. Even a block of steel would be crushed thinner by the seven tons at the bottom.

But an egg would not even be cracked.

Air is the most easily compressible of substances, and water the least compressible, far less so than the hardest metal. The weight that pushes down on the water at the bottom makes it little denser than the water at the top of the same temperature.

An egg is liquid in a porous shell, much like a human being. Unlike an egg, a human has numerous pockets of air that could let him be crushed in an instant were they not pressurized and pushing out with equal force. In Colin's gear all these forces were kept in precarious balance, and he moved warily through the water.

Suddenly an apparition. A great greenish shape. Colin hesitated. The creature slowly turned, its luminous underside lighting its ghastly form, visible as no more than form against the blackness. It began to circle about him.

It was the shark. With no air bladder it had no cavities to be crushed as it descended, no compressed air to suddenly explode or bubble as it rose. It traveled across the thermocline with impunity, and the species born in the

116

depths developed a luminescent hide to further aid its survival.

Now it broke its pattern to veer toward him and this time there were no rocks to hide behind, only the empty void. He backed away hoping to be lost in the darkness, but still the shark came, relying on senses far more keen than sight.

Colin froze, but still the shark attacked.

In desperation Colin slammed the spear gun at it. The shark rolled on its side, wrenched the gun out of Colin's hands, crushed it easily, and swam off and disappeared.

Colin was now weaponless, primitive man without the simplest tools.

Other forms were now visible—long luminescent ropes dangling before him, inches thick, studded with countless tentacles, and writhing as if dangled by a giant puppeteer. He kicked away and looked up along their length. Above him a dead fish was entangled in the ropes, and the tentacles were slowly inching the fish upward to an immense mouth.

Then the area above the mouth began to glow, an immense umbrella thirty feet across with luminous red bands like tiger stripes, and pale spots about the rim like a pearl necklace.

Though giant, the creature was filmy and pulsated gently. It was a jellyfish, a grotesque giant of the species of the shallows. Half-disintegrated fish writhed in the ghostly bell as the jellyfish churned them in its digestion.

It was as natural for the creature to be thirty feet across in the abyss as to be a few inches in the shallows. A creature evolves to the size that most naturally allows it to survive, and here where prey passed by happenstance this particular predator trapped them most easily by being a giant.

Conversely, the most likely prey survive best when only a few inches long.

Colin backed off farther, carefully avoiding the drifting tentacles. He turned about.

Several anglerfish swam by, cousins of the mini-monster Colin saw through the porthole. Their evil-looking jaws were half the size of their bodies, and their cruel expression was enhanced by long, curved sharp fangs. They swam slowly and clumsily with their mouths open. Their skins, like lizard hides, had rough folds, warts, and strange growths like clusters of eggs or strings of beads that glowed in various colors. Other growths were the strangest of all, shriveled mates attached for life.

In the timeless homeless abyss, love was unknown and even sex a product of cruelty. The male that happened upon a female sank his fangs into her flesh, drank in her blood and merged it with his. Gradually his lips and mouth fused with her skin. Eventually all his organs wasted away except for the reproductive ones, and he stayed for life as a shriveled appendage.

Now an angler crossed Colin's path demonstrating the source of its name. On an upright pole on its back it dangled a long line with a light at the end. It waved the pole back and forth, casting its line expertly until it attracted a small fish, worked its prey close, opened its mouth wide and sucked in the victim.

A tail with a red light dangled from a huge pelican-bill mouth, and that was the complete creature, a mouth and a tail.

Creatures were reduced to brainless essentials, to devouring and excretion, to the stark savagery that had been dressed in the shallows with grace and form and color.

Now, not even that. Darkness again, stretching for all space and time, yawning to infinity and yet crushing down upon Colin. The darkness seemed to reach through his eyes to his brain, squashing three hundred million years of thought, and then reaching beyond that to throat and voice, pulverizing cells beneath its weight.

He heard himself beg for light, the smallest glow to show he was not alone in the universe, to show there was a universe at all.

Then he saw a soft yellow light coming closer, gentle and reassuring. The sea was offering him a candle, a sign she had not forgotten him.

Gratefully he reached for it, and suddenly the water was turned to foam by the fury of the monster Colin had disturbed. Luminous fangs snapped and slashed about him. It was a sea dragon, a five-foot version of the tiny anglers he had seen and dreaded meeting full-size, as fearsome as its legendary namesake, but no land dragon boasted such weapons. Its eyes were huge binoculars with their own blue lights to focus on prey. Its huge mouth yawned open revealing rows of luminous spikes, the greatest of them barbed fangs, and its jaw had the heavy muscles to give it a vicious snap and bite.

The yellow light dangled from the end of a long sensitive whisker, and as it whipped back and forth it sent the creature into yet greater fury.

Its fangs took a slash out of Colin's suit before he could back away, and it wheeled about for a second pass. Colin pumped his legs frantically, struggling for breath, overstraining his breathing apparatus, and his whole body was afire for want of air.

The dragon followed, caught up, slashed again. Colin began to bleed, and his body ached as it had not since land. Exhausted, it no longer responded when he tried to propel himself. It was a heavy weight, dragging him down.

He was drifting helplessly toward the great dangling tentacles of the jellyfish. He could see the thousands of stinging cells, the tiny hairs projecting from each stinger. He need only brush past one hair of one cell. It would cling and catch him, and while he tried to shake it off it would be shooting countless barbed threads through his skin. The pain of that alone would be excruciating, but each thread contained a drop of paralyzing poison to cripple him, and make his whole body inflamed as it had never been. He would scream for death, but his brain would be the last to die and would be conscious long enough to sense his body being pulled up slowly along those tentacles to that great gaping mouth.

So this was what the Siren had brought. She had tempted him with brief liberation, and brought him death. Later she would shed false tears over his rotting bones.

He cursed the sea and all the creatures in it as the dragon came at him, its mouth opening to vast size, its luminous fangs erect giving Colin clear view of his doom. And behind him the tentacles dangled closer, almost seeming to reach forward in expectation.

"Not yet! Not yet!"

With a last desperate effort he wrenched himself out of

the way. The dragon could not turn in time and touched one of those poisonous ropes. In an instant it was in a paroxysm of pain and rage, trying to work that tentacle off, stretching it so taut it seemed it must soon break. But now countless slivers of poison were shooting into the fish, and as it thrashed about it succeeded only in wrapping more tentacles about itself, and each added its own barbs and poison. The dragon gave one final agonized convulsion and was dead. Then, slowly, those living ropes began inching the dead victim upward into its filmy bell.

And that sea dragon might have been Colin. He watched the luminous churnings of its digestion as he drifted away, or it drifted from him, he could not tell which. Finally it vanished into the distance and again the darkness closed in upon him, with nothing to tell him where the salvation of the surface lay.

The surface.

It lay miles above . . . or below . . . or to the left or right . . . in some direction somewhere, offering him glorious light, solid land beneath his feet, definable space, a living universe . . . and air.

He had renounced the land. He had turned his back on his heritage of three hundred million years, and now, fooled by the Siren, he would die while she laughed or wept false tears.

Moreover, he would die slowly, exhausting the air he had renounced, reminded moment by moment of his folly as he dangled in darkness while he gasped for dwindling bits of oxygen.

The only sound would be his desperate breathing and the gurgling of the bubbles as they fled from this madman to the freedom of the surface.

. . . to the surface . . .

The bubbles were rising to the surface! He could not see them but he could feel them. They could be his guide. The land had given him a final chance, a tiny crutch, and gratefully he grasped at it. Reaching his hand out, he felt the bubbles escaping, offering him their guidance as they rose. He rested until he could move, however feebly, then followed them upward.

How long would it take him to reach the surface, obeying the rules of ascent and going no faster than they?

Of course it was a meaningless question for there was no longer time in his existence. He was in the chaos of the waters before Creation, and perhaps he was beginning Creation all over again, rising through the eons of time as he approached the surface.

Surely he would be so paralyzed by then he would have to crawl ashore, just like the first amphibian.

Never mind.

He would leave the sea and never look back. There would be all the air in the atmosphere to breathe, around the globe and a hundred miles above it. Down here there were only the precious few bits in his tanks and mask, his lungs and sinuses, and a few molecules in the cavities in his teeth.

He felt for the bubbles again, and the compressed tiny dots tickled his fingers as they rose. A good sign the air was condensed enough to resist the outside pressures, and would last a good long while.

In fact, air was so much more compressible than water that at this depth it was packed denser than the water. Were there enough of it, he could float on it. He thought of the various advantages of air, praising it as he drifted upward, feeling those tiny bubbles that would grow larger as they ascended and . . .

. . . denser than the water . . .

His thoughts suddenly stopped, focused together on one point. The bubbles were denser than the water, which meant they were heavier, which meant they weren't rising but sinking!

And he was following them. The air in his tanks and mask, his lungs and sinuses, and even the tiny bits in his cavities were all anchors dragging him down.

His mind staggered and grew confused, no more capable than his body had been.

Now it refused to work for him, betrayed him. His ears heard an astonishing sound, the singing that drew him into the sea and was now pulling him to his death at the bottom. His eyes deceived him, let him see a single bubble glowing in this infinite blackness, and expanding instead of shrinking as the pressure increased.

The singing grew louder as that great green bubble became a circle, growing larger and larger yet until it began to reach for him.

He fought to get away, weakly kicked his crippled legs, but it encircled him and finally swallowed him.

He managed one last scream . . .

20 He was inside a cave bathed in a soft green light, and its source was everywhere, or nowhere, from beyond its walls.

He looked about him, searched for the way he had come, but he was enclosed completely.

Then he heard a voice. It was his own and it whispered inside him.

He thought of himself naked and free in the depths as any sea creature and began to feel a strange compulsion to be so.

He removed his gloves and felt the water was surprisingly warm. He realized now he was perspiring under the heavy insulation, and his wounds were no longer bleeding.

He removed more, the rubber, the foam lining, all but the mask and tanks.

The water was the temperature of his body, a comforting warmth that reminded him of childhood.

This woven raiment of nights and days,
Were it once cast off and unwound from me . . .

Again that voice whispered, asked him to give himself, to take off his skin, renounce his human shell and let the spirit within him go free. He thought of that spirit merging with the spirit of the sea and bringing him new life in death.

Naked and glad would I walk in thy ways,
Alive and aware of thy ways and thee . . .

The compulsion was now maddening. He watched his hands in amazement for they seemed to carry a life of their own as they reached for the final thread to his human life, the breathing mask. Terrified, forcing his will to its highest, he managed to regain control of his hands in time.

He knew he was going insane, that "rapture of the deep," his brain degenerating.

He tried to escape, but the cave was not much bigger than himself, and if there were an escape he would surely have seen it.

He looked at his air gauge, well into the danger area and dropping.

Again the voice whispered, and again he imagined himself in the depths, breathing water as easily as any fish. He would swim among palaces of corals and pearls, where the sun went at night and the fishes caught its glory . . .

His crawling brain fumbled with concepts he knew were mad. Lungs cannot breathe water.

And yet . . .

Water itself did not kill, nor air itself give life. They were both merely fluids, merely media for vital oxygen. Drowning was really suffocation, the water blocking oxygen from the lungs. Were there enough oxygen in the seawater he might conceivably breathe that.

Again the voice called.

But there was almost no oxygen here, not in the depths of Hades. In air of the surface, one part in five; here, as little as one part in five thousand. It was insane, and he was insane.

The gauge approached the empty mark, and he started gasping. Again the voice whispered and offered him the freedom of the sea.

> *But thou, thou art sure, thou art older than earth;*
> *Thou art strong for death and fruitful of birth . . .*

His mind raced feverishly. One part in five thousand . . . but it was the pressure that mattered, not the amount. Three pounds per square inch, that pressure forced the oxygen through the air cells and into the blood.

One part in five thousand, but it was at considerably

higher pressure, seven and a half tons. Could one compensate for the other?

The gauge reached the empty mark, and crossed it.

His mind moved more slowly, fumbled.

... seven and a half tons ... multiply by two thousand ... two ... seven ... fif ... fifteen ... Fifteen what? ...

He had to start again.

... Fifteen ... fifteen thousand pounds ... square inch ... one part oxygen in ... five thousand ... therefore ... divide five thousand into fifteen thousand . . . cancel zeroes ...

He floundered with children's arithmetic as blackness crept in at the far sides of his vision. He crawled toward the answer, reached for it, closed his hands firmly around it.

Three ... 3 ... 3 ... All he saw was that number. At this depth the pressure of oxygen was three pounds per square inch. At this depth he could breathe the sea.

Thy depths conceal and thy gulfs discover ...

Reaching up, he wrenched off his mask and tanks and now stood naked in the sea. He watched them float away and trembled as he did when he first faced that solid glass barrier. He hesitated, trembled before the barrier, then he plunged toward it. He breathed the sea.

From the first thou wert; in the end thou art.

The water rushed in through the throat and voice box, snaked around the labyrinths of the air passages, dividing as the windpipe itself divided and subdivided, branching out to reach all parts of the lungs, crushing cells and capillaries, filling craters in his joints to bursting, puffing his skin up in blisters, corroding membranes in saltwater. Each cell, gland, vessel screamed as it died, each a living thing, billions upon countless billions dying as he gasped, choked, drowned.

An insanity!

Desperately he reached again for the air tanks.

It was like the time long before when he floundered in the water for the first time and reached for his crutches.

Now the voice asked him again to give up these crutches, to reach beyond sanity, to breathe the substance with which the most powerful magic was worked, the medium of chaos and creation, the universal solvent and therefore the caldron of all substances on the planet including those of life itself, the vessel of the spirit of God, the ultimate paradox.

He gave up this last crutch to give himself completely, though it seemed like dying.

His mind called out that invocation in its last moments of awareness, "Set free my soul . . . as . . . thy . . ."

And he died.

Once more stillness was added to the vast stillness. The processes of life stopped. Time itself stopped.

And yet . . .

Time could not stop for it had never begun. This deepest part of the sea was beyond the grasp of all things by which time is perceived, the light and dark of days, the cold and warmth of the seasons, the shifting of the tides, and even the subtler changes that measure eons. There was only time outside time, the eternal night and cold, the chaos before Creation, akin to death.

But not quite death. In the sea there is no true death, for life is implicit in death just as death is implicit in life. Each thing lives from the day it dies just as it dies from the day it lives, part of an infinite chain that circles about and comes back to its beginnings.

The outer shell was dead, but there was an inner life substance, a spirit protoplasm that once related man to the beasts of the forest and made them brothers. It tied the smallest particles in the smallest drop of water to the universe in slow cosmic dance. It joined atoms to galaxies, molecules to stars, and for a long while in the outer life of this one particular shell it had been slowly unchained, and it now began to stir in those great slow rhythms.

That spirit protoplasm touched the larger spirit that was once called Nephe, Naimu, Oannes, the Spirit of God upon the waters, or simply the sea. Then, stirred by that great force, in turn it stirred each tiny cell, each of the minute billions of creatures that together formed the wondrous small universe that was once called a human being, albeit a crippled, scarred, and imperfect one. Each cell obeyed and returned along the infinite circle to its beginnings until finally that dead outer shell stirred, responded, and returned.

It was warmed and nourished in the saline solution that is the caldron of all the life-giving substances on earth, the bringer of rebirth in baptism, the worker of the most powerful magic, the most common element and rarest wonder. It bathed in the same sea as its ancient aquatic ancestor. Thus was present tied to past as time to timelessness, inner space to outer space, and oneness to allness.

And so a circle closed.

21 The abyss was miles beyond the reach of the sun, yet a glimmering like a morning glow emanated about a grotto. Colin poked his head out its mouth and looked about at the sea, eyes wide with a child's wonder. He pulled himself out and finally emerged completely, naked and free.

Like a colt stretching new legs, he stretched new muscles, new responses. He heard new sounds, felt new sensations near and distant through new senses.

He looked about him. The sea floor and rocks were lined with luminescent corals, flowers that were really animals growing on great long stalks, each seeming to pass on a flickering to the next, so that lights swept among them like windwaves through a wheatfield.

A constellation fish swam near, a creature glowing in the cosmic patterns for which it was named.

A lantern fish shone with a hundred flashing lights, each winking on and off independently, and all together forming a dazzling spectacle. Colin chased after it, caught it easily, tugged at its tail, and the lights sparkled more excitedly. He released it as he saw yet another creature to excite his wonder.

A squid jetted ahead, pulsing like an opening and closing umbrella. Its tiny tentacles were decked with little stars of splendid colors. He touched the squid, and it squirted out a cloud of ink as it scooted away, not black ink, but white, glowing, luminous. And that luminous ink was itself composed of miniature sparkles.

Then an even stranger more beautiful creature, the Venus's girdle, a long transparent belt, filmy and diaphanous, rolling and unrolling as it swam, with intricate luminescent patterns on its side. Colin touched it and that part glowed in blazing blue-white. He drew his finger through it, tracing little curlicues of fire all along its side.

He saw a dragonfish opening and closing its luminous fanged mouth in expectation of some meal, sporting a yellow lamp atop a mast, dangling a red one from a long chin whisker. Prior terror was forgotten as he mischievously stroked its whisker and the creature wheeled toward him in a rage. Colin neatly kicked out of its way and the dragon brushed against the corals which burst into glowing colors all over again in their irritation.

He turned his mind to those sounds of the sea that blended into music. On land, only the tiny organs within ears could receive those vibrations, but here his whole body heard, amplified a thousand times so that the most distant sounds seemed beside him. He felt the deepest notes, the subtleties of the great internal waves, the slow rise and fall of mountains of water within water hundreds of feet high, the low fundamentals for all the rhythms of the sea. His body swayed to it, anxious, impossible to restrain.

He swept forward in his exhilaration, dived to the bottom, then up again. His legs were light and powerful, his arms were wings to steer and bank. He could shoot as far and fast as he wished and turn in an instant, or he could plane upward and swerve down. The body that once sagged beneath him now molded itself to his bidding, elongating to a sleek arrow, or taking a curve by becoming the curve itself. He could glide in a giant circle, or a small one in which he could chase his own feet.

His body no longer his prison responded to his slightest wish. As he coasted down the sides of the great waves, or flew above their crests, countless tiny suspended creatures were stirred into light, marking his path in glowing green. He crossed his luminescent trail, spinning as he went, forming a spiral behind him, and soon the sea was painted in radiant scrolls.

He raced with the sea creatures, darting easily ahead, twisting neatly out of reach of the jellyfish's dangling tresses, dancing circles about all of them. He delighted in their amusement and ignored their irritation, a prankish child of the sea, glorying in a freedom he had never known.

Inevitably, though, he tired. He wanted other games that went deeper, that held hidden corners and surprising turns. The dark places were more exciting than the light.

He looked above him to that darkness of miles, but it was overwhelmingly fearsome.

Still, something was drawing him away. Perplexed, he tried to look beyond the darkness.

A new music enveloped him, a singing by the spirit that had guided him here. It gave him comfort and reassurance that he was a child of the sea and no harm would come to him.

For a moment he drew back, distrusting, but the song sang to him of his powers, and that he would be given a guide through that long night's travel.

There was a small eel with silver scales and glowing lights, with membranes of reflectors and lenses that could focus its lights into bright blue beams. He took the eel in hand to guide his way, and gave one nostalgic last look to the glowing garden and the colors he was leaving behind. Then he swam up toward that coldness, leaving a glowing trail behind that faded after him.

Past grotesque anglers, flying sea cucumbers, and the luminescent shark. Because water pervaded his lungs the pressures were no hindrance. He caught the crests of the internal waves to take him over the crags and peaks of the miles-high canyon, guided by his living blue light. He had dim remembrance of all these as perilous obstacles and fearsome enemies. How strangely trifling and innocuous they seemed now.

The sand river still tumbled over its great precipice, the volcanoes still lighted the distance like so many sunsets, and at last the darkness of the sea began to lighten as he came to a blue-green dawn.

He came to a place where the water shimmered like the heat waves above a fire. The silver eel wriggled frantically as he approached, afraid to cross that line. Sadly he let the eel free and watched it slither its long way back to its deep-sea home. He thought of following, but the insistent notes returned and pulled him on through steadily warming waters.

At last he reached the crest of the canyon. The colors lightened further to a gold-green, and soon he saw the rays of sunlight. He heard new sounds of creatures barely remembered, and one acutely remembered.

He went on until he saw her. Ripples ran down her soft body as she swam, and the bubbles that flowed from her trailed like a bridal train in the wind.

She saw him and came to a frightened halt in a flurry of foam. Trembling, she backed away. He swam after her and caught her easily. He stroked her and she recognized the touch of his hand and rolled her head beneath it. Then they touched noses and wrapped arms about each other and spun in a foam of bubbles.

They swam together, they played games a while, and then Colin decided to relive the old memories, this time through keener senses.

They came first to the place of color and diverse life, where tiny animals had grouped themselves into sculptures, and the fish had been so blindingly vivid it seemed a child had run amok with a paint set among them.

It was not now the way he remembered it. The reefs were denuded, blank white skeletons. Here and there were some grayish or dull-green fuzzy growths, but all else was gone. He swam bewilderedly along the remains of the reef, trying to find signs of life.

Then he did, in abundance. He remembered the starfish with nineteen arms, the crown-of-thorns with its orange spines and yellow suckers wrapping itself about the coral. Now there were dozens, hundreds, thousands of them, moving in columns like an army, leaving behind them the bleached skeletons of the corals.

Once the corals had eaten the starfish larvae, had kept down their numbers, but something had weakened the corals so that now the starfish could take their vengeance. There were armies of them now, unstoppable, killing the corals and with them the moray eel, the lion-fish, the leopard-spotted snail, the blue and gold sea bass.

He reached for one starfish, tried to pull it off the reef

and suddenly reeled back, his whole body afire. The spines had penetrated his hands and they carried venom.

He gasped and retched until the pain finally passed. He searched among fragments of shells until he found one sharp enough to serve as a blade. He stabbed at the starfish, cutting them in two, one after another, up and down the reefs until he must have slain hundreds. Then he sank exhausted, and looked at the task remaining. There were more thousands, many more than one man could ever kill.

Behind him the slain halves were twitching, starting to regenerate, to become whole new starfish.

He heard her cry, calling to him in pain. Her head hurt and she felt strangely cold in these warm waters. Worried, he guided her on.

The waters carried a strange distaste, as if grown stale or aged.

They came finally to the gold forest, or what was once a forest. Now the waters were desolate, with some shriveled remains of the trees floating on the surface. Here and there was a stray perch, a single abalone, a clutch of leafless stringy fronds, and even these were dying.

What was happening?

They swam on, searching for the forest until finally they came to its border. It was marked by another plague, countless hundreds of what were seemingly curled-up porcupines, or purple pincushions, with spines in constant motion. He remembered them as sea urchins, cousins of the starfish.

He swam down to look closely at one. Its mouth held tiny ratlike teeth in a circle, and these chewed on the little sucker disks that anchored the kelp to the rocks. These were the tasty parts to the urchin and when it had chewed them through, a hundred-foot frond was cast adrift. Colin could hear the shrieks of all the creatures in that home—barnacles, crabs, shrimp, garibaldi, sea otters—floating away to die as the frond died.

He was about to grab at the urchin, but its sharp spines instinctively made him hold off. There were hundreds more, many more than he could kill.

The balances were awry almost as if some force had

tipped the globe on end and all things had fallen the wrong way.

All would be well as soon as they found living waters.

But the waters grew more bitter, more rusted, as they swam. Day by day as they searched the sea forests her pains worsened. Her skin itched ferociously from every inch of its surface. The slightest motion of her legs sent up sharp grating pains. When she returned to the surface for air, her deep breaths set her lungs burning. Her whole body was a torment.

She could no longer hunt for herself and so he caught what occasional fish he could find and fed her, but she could barely swallow, nor long keep down what she could swallow.

He had felt her pain, and now he felt her panic. He tried to warm her when she felt cold, soothe her when she shook, bring her to pockets of cold water when she felt hot. His helplessness deepened his suffering for her. He could only hold her as he swam on, searching.

They were in coastal waters now, starved and devoid of life. The sea was a dirty brown, almost black. Suspended particles floated in the water, a black snowfall parodying the white snowfall of the long-gone plankton. The rocks on the bottom were coated with a soft gray slime, as were the stringy remains of anemones, sea cucumbers, mussels. A single bass lay choking on the bottom, its once iridescent scales darkened to a pallor. Below its gills was a strange redness like a burn.

As Colin swam, the water oozed through his fingers like syrup, and he felt his lungs burning. He looked above him. A school of herring floated upside down, their bloated bellies to the sky, and about their gills were those same red burn marks. Birds lay floating and dead, their feathers soaked in blackish tar.

He continued on, passing dead or dying crayfish, mullet, sheepshead.

Then he found the reasons. Directly above him, a forest of drilling platforms and ships leaking oil. Beyond, a river of sludge and poisons emptying into the bay. Below, oddly shaped cylinders, rusting oil drums bearing emblems of the military or the chemical companies. Several were leaking, and even as Colin watched, the current was picking up these particles along with the ooze in which they lay, sending them down the path Colin had just come, eventually to reach the forests and reefs of all oceans.

The sea was dying and she was dying. Colin knew as they rested in the shallows.

Suddenly a sharp convulsion wrenched her out of his grasp. She shook violently and uncontrollably, stirring up the black snowfall.

Even as he reached for her again to hold her, she gave one loud cry as her body lurched in a great seizure. Her back arched up in a convulsion that must surely have broken her spine, and she spun forward, flippers spread stiffly.

Suddenly there was no movement at all.

Her quiet form drifted slowly to the surface.

At first he dared not approach.

Her flippers were stiff and lifeless, her eyes frozen. The little tail still peeked out ludicrously between her hind flippers. The fur was still smooth and soft beneath his fingers as he stroked her. He shivered at her coldness, and then saw around her neck that same large red burn mark. To a scientist, a bacteria disease carried in polluted water, but Colin knew the cause if not the name. The pain fell full upon him. His desolation finally found voice, and in the sea a child wept.

Finally he looked about him. He could not bury her here. He carefully pulled her down from the surface and swam with her, coming at last to a remote place, where fish still swam, anemones still waved their tentacles, and the white snowfall still drifted.

Here he buried her, knowing that though lost to him she would be restored to the sea as a part of the sea.

He smoothed her grave carefully and slumped as the child within him died.

When at last he arose, the playfulness, the innocence, the trust had gone out of his eyes. In their stead were cunning, hatred, vindictiveness. He was an adult again.

22 The drill was set into a metal plate on the seabed, and as Colin swam about it he saw the shaft was perfectly vertical, exactly aligned with the platform above. There was sufficient scrap metal lying about the bottom, and he picked up a heavy iron bar, inserted it under the plate and pried up one corner.

The drill suddenly began squealing as though in pain. He pushed harder and the squeal grew louder and higher until it was a screech, but Colin did not stop. The rotating suddenly halted and there was a rumbling of straining gears. Suddenly the shaft was sheared apart, caught between the twisting machinery above and the obstruction beneath. Then the whole shaft assembly came toppling down into the water.

Soon he had obliterated a whole grove of the metal trees, and turned his attention to the river that emptied into the harbor.

He swam upstream amidst swirls and pools of yellow-brown films, bluish algae, whitish powders, and clumps of foam like miniature icebergs. They blocked much oxygen, but still he pulled himself on, exhausted and gasping, until he came to a building of soot-covered brick with the most noxious effluents. Another memory returned, and this one made him twinge. It was once his building.

Streamers of brown filaments flapped sluggishly as they dangled from the outlet pipes, and other fungus growths covered the floor in a thick, greasy rug. His eyes tearing, his head groggy, he still managed to pile heavy rocks into the outlet pipes. Now the chemicals spurted out in miniature fountains, and he cut the flow down further with smaller rocks until he had the pipes completely stopped.

He waited, and soon there was an explosion in the plant as the effluents backed up, blowing out machinery.

Above, the roar quieted and the smoke thinned as the plant died.

He swam farther upriver, repeating the process at each outlet pipe until his body quivered. At last, almost paralyzed from the exhaustion and poison, he let the river take him back to the sea. He had done his job well, and satisfied that he had saved the sea he drifted in the soothing currents knowing he would soon breathe living waters again. He let himself lose track of time.

He heard the noise of machinery and groggily looked above to see the drills restored, the noises of their operation at full volume, and there were more than before. Like the starfish, in killing one he had caused two to be born. He looked behind him and the chemical plants were again pouring smoke into the sky and residues back into the sea. He looked beyond them to the land and the city. Many factories, mills, cars. Like the starfish and urchins they were indestructible.

Helpless, numbed, he sank back into the water and drifted until the fresher seas cleaned out his lungs and revived him, but it did not help his deeper exhaustion.

He sat a long time by her grave, while about him the life of the sea continued in ignorance.

The shark came and saw him, came close and tasted the water about him with its pores. It sensed his suffering and began its slow calculating circle.

Colin watched stoically. Let it be now, for he was helpless. Let the shadow take his pointless life and end it.

> *Save me and hide me with thy waves,*
> *Find me one grave of thy thousand graves . . .*

The shark closed its first circle and started its second, drawing its web tighter. Soon Colin would pass into the spirit of the shark, and then into the spirit of the sea herself. The sea would live a while yet and he would know that feeling of all-being until the sea herself died.

The shark closed its final circle and then turned out of it, coming directly toward Colin, opening its jaw wide, ready to take him, and Colin was ready.

Those pure cold populous graves of thine,
Wrought without hand in a world without stain . . .

Suddenly the shark veered, picking up the scent of a blood trail, a wounded creature elsewhere more immediately tempting. It swam off and was soon lost in watery space.

He pondered, then he understood.

He swam back beyond the urchins of the kelp forest, the starfish of the coral reefs, to the edge of the great canyon.

There were rivers of mud and gravel piling up behind boulders, unstable dams that would break from time to time and go roaring down the miles-high mountain, gouging out channels as they went, a force of unbelievable power before diminishing to a gentle sandfall, and settling at the bottom.

But suppose all these rivers were to be set free simultaneously, to loosen whole sides of the mountain at once?

Bracing himself against solid ground, manipulating improvised levers, Colin cleared away rock after rock, setting free gravel rivers that roared over the side, and soon their combined force was so great they broke off jagged outcrops to make them huge rolling boulders that in turn set free other rivers.

Multiples built upon multiples, and soon the entire great canyon seemed to give way, roaring down the miles with a sound like the echoing roll of summer thunder magnified a thousandfold. The sound raced swiftly in the dense medium of the sea, scattering the numerous sea creatures to safe distances.

Finally the avalanche reached bottom and rolled across the seabed, pushing away a mass of water.

The mass flowed upward, squeezed by the canyon into a concentrated force. It passed the top of the canyon and sent Colin flying backward. He floundered, flailed his arms and legs to regain his balance, much like that first time he entered the ocean, and for some moments he was no longer the master of the sea.

But this time he was laughing.

The force reached the surface and exploded as a white hill of froth. And a great ripple was discharged from it in an everwidening circle. The ripple was certainly too small to be readily noticed in the great expanse of the sea, only a foot high, yet there was something different about it, perhaps a hint of the murderous energy locked within.

The ripple raced to the open sea, to the playground of infant waves created by many different winds. There was no pattern or order to them as they were blown about this way and that. But now this new wave passed through, notably different. It was no bigger than the others, but it was relentless, overtaking other waves, swallowing them, leaving them behind.

The wave rolled on many miles to where dark rough waters met smooth and light, and the currents swept all life together in a band of foam called a current rip. Everything at or near the surface was pulled toward this white ribbon. Trees and plants carrying shore life from some far-off islands were brought here, and about them leaped dozens of dolphins breaking the surface in endless series of arcs, taking up the feast that lay below.

The wave passed through, distracted the dolphins who sensed this wave was not ordinary. They ducked as it rolled the logs about and upset the surface life. They looked curiously as it traveled on. After a while the frightened fish below the surface resumed their feeding, and the dolphins resumed their feeding upon them.

On either side of the current rip, the waters had been swept bare and were a deep and rich blue. Beautiful and clear to human eyes, the waters were actually desolate, and blue is the color of deserts in the sea. The wave traveled on in these too-warm waters, undisturbed and undisturbing.

At last after countless miles, the waters cooled and turned green with life. In the air above fluttered swallow-like birds who made their home here thousands of miles from land. These storm petrels paddled on the water or skimmed above it, crying in excitement at the squid and crustaceans just below.

The small strange wave barely distracted birds undisturbed by storms at sea. They paddled a bit faster to stay in place as the wave passed.

It rolled on for many more miles, slowly growing by inches until its back caught the wind like an open sail. The wind lifted the wave higher, sharpened its rounded top to a ridge.

A school of small silvery fish sped toward the surface, racing ahead of the wave. Suddenly they broke through the surface, spread out fins as long as their bodies while whipping their tails on the water. Their whole bodies shook, and then they rose above the surface in great long glides, and so they were called flying fish.

The wave pushed on below them and soon was alone again, a solitary rolling promontory on a smooth sea, still giving little hint of its power. But after an extended childhood its growth would be ominously swift. It was coming upon the steeply rising floor of the continental shelf, the submerged land that rimmed the continent like a pedestal. As the deeper part of the wave stumbled upon it, it blew tresses of seaweed aside as if by a gust of wind.

As the wave was dragged back and slowed, its momentous energy was diverted upward, and so it began an ominous new growth.

In the depths, a school of herring was lifted bodily as if by many invisible hands acting in concert. They were swung in a circle and gently dropped as the force passed.

On the surface the wave slowed further and grew larger.

In the depths the breeze was now a wind, tumbling small scallops and starfish, setting sea urchins rolling like tumbleweeds. Still growing.

Sponges and barnacles that were ordinarily cemented to rocks and not dislodged by the currents this time were torn from their anchoring places.

On the surface the wave was now a size to swamp smaller boats.

In the depths, rocks were picked up by the wind of water which had become almost a gale. The rocks went somersaulting across the bottom, dislodging other rocks in a strange uphill landslide.

On the surface the wave approached the forest of drilling

platforms. It slowed further as it grew, as if conserving its strength for one purpose and seeing that purpose at hand.

In the depths, huge boulders were picked up by the hurricane and swept into the body of the wave.

Now it came to the harbor where the funnel shape squeezed the wave smaller, multiplied its fury and sent it towering higher. It approached the drilling towers and for one incredible instant it stood rock still, all its forces in precarious balance, as if steeling itself for that moment, the purpose of these thousands of miles, and of its entire life.

First the tip rolled down the front of the wall of water while the wind spread out the foam before it like a bridal veil. The tip grew bigger as it descended, as the rest of the wave rolled down behind it in a rounded curl, and that whole great tower of water began to topple.

Against that, mere metal towers were puny. They folded and buckled as if bowing in recognition of that greater power, and then towers and platforms were all swept into the great wave.

Now, with increasing speed and noise, rolling forward in an ever-thickening curl, the wave roared onto the shore, sweeping away breakwaters, docks, ships. It rolled upriver to the plants and mills, using its last energies upon them. Chimneys toppled like toothpick towers and a rain of bricks fell with the water upon each roof, blowing walls outward and spewing pipes, machines, vats, and electronic gear in a strange thick soup.

Its task done, its energy spent, and its form broken, the flattened water retreated back to the sea, taking with it innumerable bits of stone, wood, glass, and metal. It left behind scars in the sand, foundations, odd scraps, and half-buried remnants.

There was a long cemetery quiet and then the normal gentle waves rolled in. They washed over the sand, soothing the scars, taking some scraps out to sea, burying others deeper in the sand.

And then the shore was clean and unmarred as it was a hundred years ago, and the only sounds now were the waves.

23 The seabed sands were convulsed by a mischievous child, churning up water, rolling in the mud. He tugged at the tail of a sea bass. He picked up a starfish and set it among some scallops, that took one look with tiny blue-green eyes across their mantles, clacked their shells together and propelled away.

A giant grouper, a disapproving elder, turned and looked with its grumpy down-turned mouth. Colin swam in front of it, imitating it with fingers in his mouth.

Through all this was a child's laughter that was certainly a strange new sound in the sea. There was only one respite, when he patted a seal's grave to reassure her she was remembered and avenged.

There was a distant mechanical humming which grew louder until it forced itself on Colin's attention. He looked about for the source and then he saw it above, bearing down upon him.

Among the menagerie Colin had met under the sea this was surely the strangest. The great spider was several feet in diameter, a large dim eye in its center, its legs spread sidewise as if tucked out of the way until needed for landing. The strand from which it dangled stretched up out of sight, beyond the rippling ceiling of the surface.

As the spider descended, two smaller brighter eyes searched the depths, and suddenly fell full upon Colin. The spider squeaked excitedly and the humming stopped. It hung motionless, and now it seemed to Colin that the squeaking was addressed to him, harsh and demanding.

Then it slithered down again, swinging toward him by its strand. He took this as a sign of attack, picked up a rock

141

and hit the spider a warning blow. All he got was a re-sounding clank. It had a tougher skin than even the shark. He struck again. Clank. Clank.

The sounds reverberated inside the spider and it squeaked again frantically.

Colin tried to get at the eyes, but after one blow the spider lowered protective eyelids. Now it was blind but impervious.

He flew above it to the strand, figuring it was the weakest part. He hit at it, and the spider shrieked in pain and panic. The humming noise began again, and the spider retreated, rising by its strand.

Colin flew up with it until just short of the surface, gave it some good parting blows with the rock, and just as it vanished thumbed his nose in goodbye.

It was night, and Colin lay sleeping, suspended comfortably in the depths.

In the distance there was a vaguely disturbing noise, a deep rumble, almost imperceptible at first but it gradually grew louder and more powerful. It gradually penetrated Colin's sleep and finally awakened him.

When he opened his eyes, his breath caught.

In the distance and coming closer were five eyes, two pairs flanking the fifth like the five markings on a playing card, and above them was a strangely lighted forehead. Only these cold white lights, a bellicose parody of his luminous deep-sea-playmates, were visible to him, but they suggested a creature of awful powers and deep hatred.

As it came closer it gave off a new sound in addition to the deep rumble, and quite unlike any other living sound of the sea: a squeal, rising and falling, a chirp of a giant bird in an immense cavern.

As the eyes came closer he discerned more of the creature. Alongside the eyes were a pair of twisting antennae with odd protuberances at their tips, and some smaller lights evidently capable of tracking their prey in any direction. From little grids at the tips came those electronic chirps that he now knew were for echo-locating him.

Then he saw something much more ominous, two great

arms or tentacles with grasping claws at the ends that now reached out for him.

It was a giant squid, and as he retreated it came after him propelled not by the jets of the squids he knew but by a powerful spinning propeller.

He swam quickly aside at the last moment. The antenna eyes came about, the howl rose, and again the light found him. The squid swung about to follow its eyes, guided by smaller propellers on its side, and rolled forward reaching its claws for him. This time they missed by inches and they snapped in frustration.

Colin tried to outswim it, twisting and turning in his path, but each time the squid matched his maneuver, turning up, down, to either side, even backing up.

He soon tired but the squid was tireless. Each time it lost him for a moment, the howl increased, the antennae turned and it found him again.

But by this time Colin noticed a weakness. Movements to the side were accomplished by spinning either of its flanking little propellers, but to change direction up or down demanded precious moments to adjust their tilt.

He found himself backed against a rock wall beneath several outcrops and ledges. There was a pause as if the squid were savoring its triumph before making its kill, and then it came bearing down.

Colin feinted to the left, the claws swung easily in that direction, and Colin suddenly scooted upward out of sight. The squid lost him for the moment, and squawked in vexation.

Colin picked a crevice with just enough room in which to squeeze himself. The ledge cut off most of his view, and he could just barely see the antennae and claws as they searched out various hiding places.

Upward, slowly upward the squid sniffed, following little overturned rocks or seemingly invisible tracks. Closer came its sound. Then it saw him, trapped in his refuge. The claws tried to tear the rocks away but to no avail. Colin could look out of a small opening in the crevice and see those strange glaring white eyes as the squid scratched at the rock in frustration.

Colin's leg dangled outside the outcrop and the squid

made a grab for it, but he pulled his leg in just in time. The claw snapped in greater rage, and worked its way dangerously into the crevice. Colin pulled down a loose rock and smashed it on the claw.

He heard a howl of outrage, and the squid withdrew. It reached its hand into a pouch on its underside, disconnected its claw and picked up a strange round peg, as if it had amputated itself and refitted a peg-arm. The squid approached again, and Colin heard a sharp whine, a grinding noise that seemed to emanate from the rock itself. He looked up at the source of the sound, knowing something new and dangerous was being done, but powerless to stop it.

The drilling stopped. The peg-arm withdrew. The intact claw inserted something into that hole, tapped it, and backed off. Then the squid retreated out of sight, and all was quiet.

Was the squid still there? Could he escape now? He listened closely for the smallest sound, and was about to escape when suddenly there was the thunder of an explosion and Colin was shoved against the rock by the concussion. The ledge was blasted into chunks and fell away.

In pain, dazed and bleeding, he could still see the squid coming straight for him. In a stupor, he picked up one of the loose chunks and charged straight for the antennae. He smashed one bright eye before a claw clamped on his leg and pulled him down. There were raucous squawks of elation as the second claw clamped his arm.

He flailed as helplessly as a raggedy doll as the squid pointed its nose up, and carried him dangling to the surface. The duck squawk, electronic howl, and rumble all melted into a cacophonous cackle of glee.

Just before breaking the surface, Colin saw a great thick net dropping over him and entangling him.

And then, nothing.

24 There was a ferment on the surface, then a white foam and the squid rose through it with a loud hiss, finally settling down and bobbing on the waves like a toy boat in a bathtub. Far from the grim silhouette it presented in water, it actually sported a rather gay yellow coat. The metal gleamed with wetness and caught the glint of the bright sun. A sporty black stripe ran down its side bearing the manufacturer's name. The bizarre antennae were instruments on swivels, a remote TV camera, a photo camera, and sonar speakers. Its eyes were portholes and spotlights, its lighted forehead an observing window, and out of water the mechanical manipulators seemed almost unwieldy. It was one of a varied fleet of highly maneuverable miniature submarines used by oceanographic explorers for inspecting, sampling, and retrieving.

There was the squeaking of a wheel turning, and the hatch swung open. A moment later the marine bioolgist stepped out and squinted at the bright daylight.

He waved and a rope swung down to him. Grabbing it he guided the submarine to the mother ship, an oceanographic research vessel, and gingerly made his way off the sub and up the accommodation ladder.

The unusual catch had attracted most the ship's crew and for a few moments they forgot about taking up the sub, or lashing down the diving bell, the spiderlike steel sphere that rested on the deck with its chain strand limp at its side.

The crew awaited impatiently the deck officer's signals to the man on the boom. It was a delicate operation for the

net had to be lined up with the special tank that was barely
larger than the catch, which even now was twisting and
writhing frantically in the net.

At the deck officer's gesture, a corner fell away and their
catch dropped with a thud onto the deck, missing the tank
by inches.

And there was one of the most grotesque creatures they
had ever seen, flailing, twisting, rolling across the flooring.
The crew yelled excited commands and countercommands
as the creature bounced its way toward the opening in the
railing, trying to get back to the sea. A deckhand was there
in time, and holding on to the rails with both hands, he
kicked the creature back.

In what seemed an almost epileptic seizure, the creature
slammed its tail onto the deck, and the shock rolled up its
body in a wave until its head hit the wood. To the biologist
it seemed the creature was trying to destroy itself and he
shouted to the others a cry that got lost in the general
ruckus. He tried to get some help in working the creature
up into the tank, but no one dared approach. Most of these
men knew, for instance, what a shark could do out of
water—and even a supposedly dead shark.

The creature gasped and its flippers shuddered with the
convulsions of its body and gills. Gradually it weakened.
The gasps were shorter, and its thuds on the deck diminished to quiverings. The crew gathered cautiously closer,
suddenly silent.

The creature's gills caught on one breath, froze, and
there was a sudden shake of its entire body. Then it
relaxed slowly as death crept upward from its shortened
webbed legs and flippers, its plumpish thickly scaled body,
and finally its strange humanoid face.

Then it was silent.

The biologist approached gingerly and touched the creature on the chest, trying to find some sign of life. He could
find nothing, but then he was not altogether certain what
he should look for.

When he looked at the clouded eyes, however, he had
an uncomfortable feeling of recognition. As grotesque as it
was, the creature suddenly seemed vaguely human, as say, a

seal is vaguely a bear, except that this creature was a water breather, perhaps having had an extra hundred million years or so to convert lungs back to gills, completing the return seemingly sought by the evolving sea mammals. But that did not answer the questions, for no completely aquatic creature had such articulated appendages, with claws that could grab and hold. Perhaps this was the legendary merman.

But then logic took hold, and the biologist dismissed his fancies. It was merely a fish.

He tried to roll the creature on its back, and then stopped. A flap of skin enclosed a paper, a page torn out of a book of poems. The creature must have accidentally snagged it in a refuse heap.

A horn sounded summoning the crew to their stations. They scratched their heads, grunted, or shrugged depending on their relative degrees of remaining interest, and left the biologist alone with his prize.

Idly, he glanced at the verses:

> *I will go back to the great sweet mother,*
> *Mother and lover of men, the Sea.*

He felt a sudden trembling, as if on the edge of some awesome revelation. He looked again at the creature, and this time he let his fancies go, let them reach for their wildest extremes, let them fly beyond this deck, this ship, let them plunge beneath the sea, beyond the shallows of gold-green kelp forests and the creatures within, beyond the coral reefs where vividly colored stone sculptures were really growing colonies of animals, to the edge of the abyss where the darkness was infinite and beyond measure and time, and then down to the depths where fish shimmered like stars against a pitch-black night, to the deepest wounds of the planet, its very birthplace, its womb where lay the ultimate mysteries of the sea and life itself, and there he saw a strange light that slowly grew toward him as he was pulled toward it.

And then he heard it, an ancient and beautiful sound, almost a singing that seemed the sum of all music and all life, the song of the sea itself . . .

The bell clanged on deck, indicating the ship was about to get under way.

He shook himself out of his reverie and looked about him, almost surprised to find himself on the ship's deck. The singing was gone, if it ever was there. There was no sound at all. The strange form lay quiet and dead.

Restless, with a vague sense of being deeply cheated of he knew not what, he walked to the railing and looked down. Points of sunlight silently burst on the surface, but he tried to look below that, miles below to the abyssal depths. But he saw nothing.

He wondered about the unknowns in the depths that would still be mysteries when his descendants would step out on the farthest planets of the solar system. Suddenly it seemed wrong to take the creature away from its home, even in death, to have it broken apart with separate organs in formaldehyde. He felt the strangest unprofessional urge to return it, to roll it over the side and let it sink slowly back to its deep-sea home, to gain its justified rest in its own burial place.

Ridicule it as he might, the urge grew until it became maddening. He looked about to make sure he was still alone on deck, then, gasping with the effort, he pulled the creature to the railing.

He looked down and saw the tiger shark following the ship. But it was too late. The ship took an unexpected roll, and the corpse fell over the edge. He reached over the railing after it—a reflex action—but of course it was a useless gesture. He could only watch helplessly as it hit the shiny glass barrier, then broke through it.

The water turned briefly white as it swirled about the form, then covered it and drew it down out of sight.

There was stillness a few moments, but then suddenly the water foamed and surged, and the biologist recoiled from the havoc he knew was taking place underneath. The creature would never reach its resting place.

So it was all for naught.

The biologist could only wonder at the strange madness

that possessed him. He wondered what his colleagues would think of him.

Then he wondered if he should tell them.

He would come to wonder about a number of things.

AUTHOR'S NOTE

Readers interested in the truth behind the fiction will find some it in the following works:

There is a general account of deep-sea explorations in *The Greatest Depths,* by Gardner Soule (Philadelphia: Macrae Smith, 1970). There are the specific feats of William Beebe in *Half-Mile Down* (Harcourt, Brace, 1934) and Jacques Piccard in *Seven Miles Down* (Putnam, 1961). Dr. Piccard's drift in the deep-sea currents was reported by *The New York Times* through the summer of 1969, and most fully on August 20.

Experiments in extended underwater living by the U.S. Navy are shown in two films, *Man in the Sea* (1966) and *Sealab One* (1965), distributed by the National Audiovisual Center, Washington, D.C. Jacques Cousteau's film on his underwater habitat, *World Without Sun* (1964), is distributed by McGraw-Hill Textfilms, New York.

Skin Diving and Exploring Underwater, by John Sweeney (McGraw-Hill, 1955), and *The Skin Diver,* by Elgin Ciampi (Ronald Press, 1960), tell of the individual diver.

The strange life in the deepest parts of the sea is documented and illustrated in Clarence P. Idyll's *Abyss* (Crowell, 1964) and William J. Cromie's *Living World of the Sea* (Prentice-Hall, 1966).

The Life of the Ocean, by N. J. Berrill (McGraw-Hill, 1966) features the more familiar life near the surface, beautifully illustrated.

The creatures can be heard in recordings on *Sounds of the Sea* (6121; Folkways Records, New York) and *Songs of the Humpback Whale* (CRM Recordings, Del Mar, California).

Information on sharks came from an article by Nathaniel T. Kenney in *National Geographic*, February 1968, and books by Jacques Cousteau (*The Shark*, Doubleday, 1970) and Thomas Helm (*Shark!*, Collier, 1963).

The life of a wild seal is movingly told in Frank S. Stuart's *A Seal's World* (McGraw-Hill, 1954).

Experiences with individual seals are recounted in Rowena Farre's *Seal Morning* (Rinehart, 1957), H. G. Hurrell's *Atlanta, My Seal* (London: W. Kimber, 1963), and in Nina Warner Hooke's *The Seal Summer* (Harcourt, Brace, 1965). Also I gratefully acknowledge helpful information provided by the Sea Mammal Motivational Institute in Wye, Maryland.

Human Animals, by Frank Hamel (New York: University Books, 1969), provides a mystical frame in which to place tales of the mermaid and her kin; also Gwen Benwell and Arthur Waugh's *Sea Enchantress* (London: Hutchinson, 1961), and for legends of the seal, David Thomson's *The People of the Sea* (London: Barrie & Rockliff, 1965).

ABOUT THE AUTHOR

ARNOLD FEDERBUSH was born in New York City in 1935. He received a B.A. from Washington Square College of New York University and an M.A. in Theater Arts from the University of California, Los Angeles. He is a film writer and film editor and wrote the screenplay adaptation of *Manchild in the Promised Land*. Mr. Federbush lives in New York City.

SPECIAL OFFER: If you enjoyed this book and would like to have our catalog of over 1,400 other Bantam titles, just send your name and address and 10¢ (to help defray postage and handling costs) to: Catalog Department, Bantam Books, Inc., 414 East Golf Rd., Des Plaines, Ill. 60016.

OUT OF THIS WORLD!

That's the only way to describe Bantam's great series of science-fiction classics. These space-age thrillers are filled with terror, fancy and adventure and written by America's most renowned writers of science fiction. Welcome to outer space and have a good trip!

☐	A CANTICLE FOR LEIBOWITZ by Walter Miller, Jr.	5423	95¢
☐	THE DAY OF THE DRONES by A. M. Lightner	5567	75¢
☐	THE MARTIAN CHRONICLES by Ray Bradbury	5613	95¢
☐	FANTASTIC VOYAGE by Isaac Asimov	7137	95¢
☐	RAGA SIX by Frank Lauria	7249	$1.25
☐	HELLSTROM'S HIVE by Frank Herbert	8276	$1.50
☐	HIERO'S JOURNEY by Sterling Lanier	8534	$1.25
☐	DHALGREN by Samuel R. Delany	8554	$1.95
☐	20,000 LEAGUES UNDER THE SEA by Jules Verne	8569	95¢
☐	ALAS, BABYLON by Pat Frank	8581	$1.25
☐	STAR TREK 10 by James Blish	8611	95¢
☐	THE MYSTERIOUS ISLAND by Jules Verne	8652	95¢
☐	THE TIME MACHINE by H. G. Wells	8783	75¢

Buy them at your local bookstore or use this handy coupon for ordering:

Bantam Books, Inc., Dept. SF, 414 East Golf Road, Des Plaines, Ill. 60016

Please send me the books I have checked above. I am enclosing $_____ (please add 35¢ to cover postage and handling). Send check or money order —no cash or C.O.D.'s please.

Mr/Mrs/Miss_____

Address_____

City_____State/Zip_____

SF—4/75

Please allow three weeks for delivery. This offer expires 4/76.

OTHER WORLDS.
OTHER REALITIES.

In fact and fiction, these extraordinary books bring the fascinating world of the supernatural down to earth from ancient astronauts and black magic to witchcraft voodoo and mysticism—these books look at other worlds and examine other realities.

☐ THE DEVIL'S TRIANGLE (8445/$1.50)—Fact

☐ POWER THROUGH WITCHCRAFT (8673/$1.25)—Fact

☐ CHARIOTS OF THE GODS (Q5753/$1.25)—Fact

☐ A COMPLETE GUIDE TO THE TAROT (Q6696/$1.25)—Fact

☐ WITCHCRAFT AND BLACK MAGIC (7996/$1.95)—Fact

☐ THE EXORCIST (X7200/$1.75)—Fiction

☐ GODS FROM OUTER SPACE (Q7276/$1.25)—Fact

☐ NOT OF THIS WORLD (7696/$1.25)—Fact

☐ GOD DRIVES A FLYING SAUCER (7733/$1.25)—Fact

☐ THE SPACESHIPS OF EZEKIEL (8378/$1.95)—Fact

Buy them at your local bookstore or use this handy coupon for ordering:

Bantam Books, Inc., Dept. OW, 414 East Golf Road, Des Plaines, Ill. 60016

Please send me the books I have checked above. I am enclosing $_____ (please add 35¢ to cover postage and handling). Send check or money order —no cash or C.O.D.'s please.

Mr/Mrs/Miss_____

Address_____

City_____ State/Zip_____

OW—4/75

Please allow three weeks for delivery. This offer expires 4/76.

RAY BRADBURY

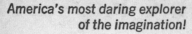

*America's most daring explorer
of the imagination!*

- ☐ MACHINERIES OF JOY — (8304—95¢)
- ☐ THE WONDERFUL ICE CREAM SUIT & OTHER PLAYS — (8297—95¢)
- ☐ TIMELESS STORIES FOR TODAY AND TOMORROW — (8162—95¢)
- ☐ MEDICINE FOR MELANCHOLY — (8098—95¢)
- ☐ DANDELION WINE — (8027—95¢)
- ☐ R IS FOR ROCKET — (7988—95¢)
- ☐ S IS FOR SPACE — (7961—95¢)
- ☐ THE ILLUSTRATED MAN — (7112—95¢)
- ☐ I SING THE BODY ELECTRIC — (6652—$1.25)
- ☐ SOMETHING WICKED THIS WAY COMES — (6438—$1.25)
- ☐ THE MARTIAN CHRONICLES — (5613—95¢)
- ☐ GOLDEN APPLES OF THE SUN — (4867—75¢)

Buy them at your local bookstore or use this handy coupon for ordering:

Bantam Books, Inc., Dept. RBS, 414 East Golf Road, Des Plaines, Ill. 60016

Please send me the books I have checked above. I am enclosing $_____
(please add 35¢ to cover postage and handling). Send check or money order
—no cash or C.O.D.'s please.

Mr/Mrs/Miss_____

Address_____

City_____ State/Zip_____

RBS—5/75

Please allow three weeks for delivery. This offer expires 5/76.

Bantam Book Catalog

It lists over a thousand money-saving best-sellers originally priced from $3.75 to $15.00 —bestsellers that are yours now for as little as 50¢ to $2.95!

The catalog gives you a great opportunity to build your own private library at huge savings!

So don't delay any longer—send us your name and address and 10¢ (to help defray postage and handling costs).

BANTAM BOOKS, INC.
Dept. FC, 414 East Golf Road, Des Plaines, Ill. 60016

Mr./Mrs./Miss_____
(please print)

Address_____

City_____ State_____ Zip_____

Do you know someone who enjoys books? Just give us their names and addresses and we'll send them a catalog too!

Mr./Mrs./Miss_____

Address_____

City_____ State_____ Zip_____

Mr./Mrs./Miss_____

Address_____

City_____ State_____ Zip_____

FC—1/75